THE CORAL ISLAND

About the author

ROBERT MICHAEL BALLANTYNE was born in Edinburgh on 24 April 1825. He died in Rome on 8 February 1894.

When he was sixteen he went to Canada, as a clerk in the Hudson Bay Company, and for six years travelled in North America, trading with the Indians. Then he returned to Scotland and worked in the printing and publishing firm of Messrs Thomas Constable of Edinburgh, where he had family connections through his uncle, who had printed Sir Walter Scott's works.

In 1855 he first tried story-telling with a book based on his own experiences in Canada called 'The Young Fur Traders'. He followed this with 'Ungrava: A Tale of Esquimaux-Land' in 1857, and in 1858 wrote his most famous book, 'The Coral Island'. "To be born is to be wrecked on an island," wrote Barrie, and declared that every boy so wrecked "wants a guide: in short 'The Coral Island.' It ought to be waiting for him when he comes." It is still the most famous 'wrecked-island' story for boys.

Ballantyne did in fact write a sequel about Ralph, Jack, and Peterkin when they were grown men, called 'The Gorilla Hunters' (1861) which didn't prove as popular as 'The Coral Island'. Of the eight books he wrote most of them based on first-hand experience, the best are those dealing with Canada and the 'Wild West' of his own early days, especially 'The Dog Crusoe' (1860) and 'The Wild Man of the West' (1863).

Besides adventure stories Ballantyne wrote and illustrated several books of verse for young children, such as 'The Robber Kitten' (1860), and he was an accomplished water-colour artist who exhibited at the Royal Scottish Academy.

R.M. Ballantyne

The Coral Island

Abridged by Olive Jones

A Thames/Magnet Book

Magnet paperback edition first published
in Great Britain 1982 by Methuen Children's Books Ltd
11 New Fetter Lane, London EC4P 4EE
in association with Thames Television International Ltd
149 Tottenham Court Road, London W1
This edition copyright © 1982
Methuen Children's Books Ltd

Photoset by Rowland Phototypesetting Ltd
Bury St Edmunds, Suffolk
Printed in Great Britain by
Cox & Wyman Ltd, Reading

ISBN 0 423 00310 0

THE CORAL ISLAND

CHAPTER I

My father was a sea-captain; my grandfather was a sea-captain; my great-grandfather had been a marine. As far back as our family could be traced, it had been intimately connected with the great watery waste. My mother always went to sea with my father on his long voyages, and so spent the greater part of her life upon the water.

Thus it was, I suppose, that I came to inherit a roving disposition. Soon after I was born, my father purchased a small cottage in a fishing village on the west coast of England, and settled down to spend the evening of his life on the shores of the sea which had for so many years been his home. It was not long after this that I began to show the roving spirit that dwelt within me. As I grew older I wandered far and near on the shore and in the woods, and did not rest content until my father bound me apprentice to a coasting vessel, and let me go to sea.

For some years I was happy in visiting the seaports, and in coasting along the shores of my native land. My Christian name was Ralph, and my comrades added to this the name of Rover, in consequence of my passion for travelling.

While engaged in the coasting trade, I fell in with many seamen who had travelled to almost every quarter of the globe; and my heart glowed within me as they recounted their wild adventures in foreign lands – the dreadful storms they had weathered, the appalling dangers they had escaped, the wonderful creatures they had seen both on the land and in the sea, and the interesting lands and strange people they had visited. But of all the places of which they told me, none captivated my imagination so much as the Coral Islands of the Southern Seas. They told me of thousands of beautiful fertile islands that had been formed by a small creature called the coral insect, where summer reigned nearly all the year round – where the trees were laden with a constant harvest of luxuriant fruit – where the climate was almost perpetually delightful – yet where, strange to say, men were wild and blood-thirsty. These exciting accounts had so great an effect upon my mind, that, when I reached the age of fifteen, I resolved to make a voyage to the South Seas.

I had no little difficulty at first in prevailing on my parents to let me go; but when I urged on my father that he would never have become a great captain had he remained in the coasting trade, he gave his consent. My mother no longer offered opposition to my wishes. 'But oh, Ralph,' she said, on the day I bade her adieu, 'come back soon to us, my dear boy, for we are getting old.'

My father placed me under the charge of an old mess-mate of his, a merchant captain, who was sailing to the South Seas in his own ship, the *Arrow*. My mother gave me her blessing and a small Bible; and her last request was that I would never forget to read a chapter every day, and say my prayers; which I promised, with tears in my eyes, that I would certainly do.

Soon afterwards I went on board the *Arrow*, which was a fine large ship, and set sail for the islands of the Pacific Ocean.

It was a bright, beautiful, warm day when our ship spread her canvas to the breeze, and sailed for the south. My heart bounded with delight as I listened to the merry chorus of the sailors, while they hauled at the ropes and got in the anchor! The captain shouted – the men ran to obey – the noble ship bent over to the breeze, and the shore gradually faded from my view.

The first thing that struck me as being different from anything I had yet seen during my short career on the sea, was the hoisting of the anchor on deck, and lashing it firmly down with ropes, as if we would require its services no more.

'There, lass,' cried a broad-shouldered jack-tar, giving the fluke of the anchor a hearty slap with his hand, 'there, lass, take a good nap now, for we shan't ask you to kiss the mud again for many a long day to come!'

There were a number of boys in the ship, but two of them were my special favourites. Jack Martin was a tall, strapping, broad-shouldered youth of eighteen, with a handsome, good-humoured face. He had had a good education, was clever and hearty and lion-like in his actions, but mild and quiet in disposition. Jack was a general favourite. My other companion was Peterkin. He was little, quick, funny, decidedly mischievous, and about fourteen years old. But Peterkin's mischief was almost always harmless, else he could not have been so much beloved as he was.

'Hallo! youngster,' said Jack Martin, giving me a slap on the shoulder, the day I joined the ship, 'come below and I'll show you your berth. You and I are to be mess-mates.'

I shall say little about the first part of our voyage. We had the usual amount of rough weather and calm; also we saw many strange fish rolling in the sea, and I was greatly delighted one day by seeing a shoal of flying-fish dart out of the water and skim through the air about a foot above the surface. They were pursued by dolphins, which feed on them, and one flying-fish in its terror flew over the ship, struck on the rigging, and fell upon the deck. Its wings were just fins elongated, and we found that they could never fly far at a time, and never mounted into the air like birds, but skimmed along the surface of the sea. Jack and I had it for dinner, and found it remarkably good.

When we approached Cape Horn, at the southern extremity of America, the weather became very cold and stormy, and the sailors began to tell stories about the furious gales and the dangers of that terrible cape.

'Cape Horn,' said one, 'is the most horrible headland I ever doubled. I've sailed round it twice already, and both times the ship was a'most blow'd out o' the water.'

'An' I've been round it once,' said another, 'an' that time

the sails were split, and the ropes frozen in the blocks, so that they wouldn't work, and we wos all but lost.'

'An' I've been round it five times,' cried a third, 'an' every time wos wuss than another, the gales wos so tree-mendous!'

'And I've been round it no times at all,' cried Peterkin, with an impudent wink of his eye, 'an' *that* time I wos blow'd inside out!'

Nevertheless, we passed the dreaded cape without much rough weather, and in the course of a few weeks were sailing gently, before a warm tropical breeze, over the Pacific Ocean. Thus we proceeded on our voyage, sometimes bounding merrily before a fair breeze, at other times floating calmly on the glassy wave and fishing for the curious inhabitants of the deep – all of which, although the sailors thought little of them, were strange, and interesting, and very wonderful to me.

At last we came among the Coral Islands of the Pacific, and I shall never forget the delight with which I gazed at the pure, white, dazzling shores, and the verdant palm trees, beautiful in the sunshine. And often did we three long to be landed on one, imagining that we should certainly find perfect happiness there!

One night, soon after we entered the tropics, an awful storm burst upon our ship. The first squall of wind carried away two of our masts, and left only the foremast standing. Even this, however, was more than enough, for we did not dare to hoist a rag of sail on it. For five days the tempest raged in all its fury. Everything was swept off the decks except one small boat. The steersman was lashed to the wheel, lest he should be washed away, and we all gave ourselves up for lost. The captain said that he had no idea where we were, as we had been blown far out of our course; and we feared much that we might get among the dangerous coral reefs which are so numerous in the Pacific. At daybreak on the sixth morning of the gale we saw land ahead. It was an island encircled by a reef of coral on which the waves broke in fury. There was calm water within this reef, but we could only see one narrow opening into it. For this opening we steered, but, before we reached it, a tremendous wave broke on our stern, tore the rudder completely off, and left us at the mercy of the winds and waves.

'It's all over with us now, lads,' said the captain to the men; 'get the boat ready to launch; we shall be on the rocks in less than half an hour.'

The men obeyed in gloomy silence, for they felt that there was little hope of so small a boat living in such a sea.

'Come, boys,' said Jack Martin, in a grave tone, to me and Peterkin, 'come, boys, we three shall stick together. You see it is impossible that the little boat can reach the shore, crowded with men. It will be sure to upset, so I mean rather to trust myself to a large oar. I see through the telescope that the ship will strike at the tail of the reef, where the waves break into the quiet water inside; so, if we manage to cling to the oar till it is driven over the breakers, we may perhaps gain the shore. What say you; will you join me?'

We gladly agreed to follow Jack, for he inspired us with confidence, although I could perceive, by the sad tone of his voice, that he had little hope; and, indeed, when I looked at the white waves that lashed the reef and boiled against the rocks as if in fury, I felt that there was but a step between us and death.

The ship was now very near the rocks. The men were ready with the boat, and the captain beside them giving orders, when a tremendous wave came towards us. We three ran towards the bow to lay hold of our oar, and had barely reached it when the wave fell on the deck with a crash like thunder. At the same moment the ship struck, the foremast broke off close to the deck and went over the side, carrying the boat and men along with it. Our oar got entangled with the wreck, and Jack seized an axe to cut it free, but, owing to the motion of the ship, he missed the cordage and struck the axe deep into the oar. Another wave, however, washed it clear of the wreck. We all seized hold of it, and the next instant we were struggling in the wild sea. The last thing I saw was the boat whirling in the surf, and all the sailors tossed into the foaming waves. Then I became insensible.

On recovering from my swoon, I found myself lying on a bank of soft grass, under the shelter of an overhanging rock, with Peterkin on his knees by my side, bathing my temples with water, and endeavouring to stop the blood that flowed from a wound in my forehead.

CHAPTER II

As I slowly recovered and heard the voice of Peterkin inquiring whether I felt better, I thought that I must have overslept, and should be sent to the mast-head for being lazy; but before I could leap up in haste, the thought seemed to vanish suddenly away, and I fancied that I must have been ill. Gradually the roar of the surf became louder and more distinct. I thought of being wrecked far, far away from my native land, and slowly opened my eyes to meet those of my companion Jack, who, with a look of intense anxiety, was gazing into my face.

'Speak to us, my dear Ralph,' whispered Jack, 'are you better now?'

I smiled and looked up, saying: 'Better; why, what do you mean, Jack? I'm quite well.'

'Then what are you shamming for, and frightening us in this way?' said Peterkin.

I now raised myself on my elbow, and putting my hand to my forehead, found that it had been cut pretty severely, and that I had lost a good deal of blood.

'Come, come, Ralph,' said Jack, pressing me gently backward, 'lie down, my boy; you're not right yet. Wet your lips with this water, it's cool and clear as crystal. I got it from a rivulet close at hand. There now, don't say a word,' said he, seeing me about to speak. 'I'll tell you all about it, but you must not utter a syllable till you have rested well.'

'Oh! don't stop him from speaking, Jack,' said Peterkin, who busied himself in erecting a shelter of broken branches to protect me from the wind; which, however, was almost unnecessary, for the rock beside which I had been laid completely broke the force of the gale. 'Let him speak, Jack; it's a comfort to hear that he's alive, after lying there stiff and white for a whole hour, just like an Egyptian mummy. Never saw such a fellow as you are, Ralph; always up to mischief. You've almost knocked out all my teeth and more than half choked me, and now you go shamming dead! It's very wicked of you, indeed it is.'

While Peterkin ran on in this style, my faculties became quite clear again. 'What do you mean by saying I half choked you, Peterkin?' said I.

'What do I mean? Don't you remember –'

'I remember nothing,' said I, interrupting him, 'after we were thrown into the sea.'

'Hush, Peterkin,' said Jack, 'you're exciting Ralph with your nonsense. I'll explain it to you. You recollect that after the ship struck, we three sprang over the bow into the sea; well, I noticed that the oar struck your head and gave you that cut on the brow, which nearly stunned you, so that you grasped Peterkin round the neck. In doing so you pushed the telescope – which you clung to as if it had been your life – against Peterkin's mouth –'

'Pushed it against his mouth!' interrupted Peterkin. 'Say crammed it down his throat. Why, there's a distinct mark of the brass rim on the back of my gullet at this moment!'

'Well, be that as it may,' continued Jack, 'you clung to him, Ralph, till I feared you really would choke him; but I saw that he had a good hold of the oar, so I exerted myself to the utmost to push you towards the shore, which we luckily reached without much trouble, for the water inside the reef is quite calm.'

'But the captain and crew, what of them?' I inquired, anxiously.

Jack shook his head.

'Are they lost?'

'No, they are not lost, I hope, but I fear there is not much chance of their being saved. The ship struck at the very tail of the island on which we were cast. When the boat was tossed into the sea it fortunately did not upset, although it shipped a good deal of water, and all the men managed to scramble into it; but before they could get the oars out the gale carried them past the point and away to leeward of the island. After we landed I saw them endeavouring to pull towards us, but as they had only one pair of oars out of the eight that belong to the boat, and as the wind was blowing right in their teeth, they gradually lost ground. Then I saw them put about and hoist some sort of sail, a blanket, I fancy, for it was too small for the boat – and in half an hour they were out of sight.'

'Poor fellows,' I murmured, sorrowfully.

'But the more I think about it, I've better hope of them,' continued Jack, in a more cheerful tone. 'You see, Ralph, I've read a great deal about these South Sea Islands, and I know that in many places they are scattered about in thousands over the sea, so they're almost sure to fall in with one of them before long.'

'I'm sure I hope so,' said Peterkin, earnestly. 'But what has become of the wreck, Jack? I saw you clambering up the rocks there while I was watching Ralph. Did you say she had gone to pieces?'

'No, she has not gone to pieces, but she has gone to the bottom,' replied Jack. 'As I said before, she struck on the tail of the island and stove in her bow, but the next breaker swung her clear, and she floated away to leeward. The poor fellows in the boat made a hard struggle to reach her, but long before they came near her she filled and went down. It was after she foundered that I saw them trying to pull to the island.'

There was a long silence after Jack ceased speaking, and I have no doubt that each was revolving in his mind our extraordinary position. For my part I cannot say that my reflections were very agreeable. I knew that we were on an island, for Jack had said so, but whether it was inhabited or not I did not know. 'Oh!' thought I, 'if the ship had only stuck on the rocks we might have done pretty well, for we could have obtained provisions from her, and tools to enable us to build a shelter, but now – alas! alas! we are lost!' These last words I uttered aloud in my distress.

'Lost, Ralph?' exclaimed Jack. 'Saved, you should have said.'

'Do you know what conclusion *I* have come to?' said Peterkin. 'I have made up my mind that it's capital – first rate – the best thing that ever happened to us, and the most splendid prospect that ever lay before three jolly young tars. We've got an island all to ourselves. You shall be king, Jack; Ralph, prime minister, and I shall be –'

'The court jester,' interrupted Jack.

'No,' retorted Peterkin, 'I have no title at all. I shall merely accept a highly responsible situation under government, for you see, Jack, I'm fond of having an enormous salary and nothing to do. We'll build a charming villa, and plant a lovely garden round it, full of tropical flowers, and we'll farm the land, plant, sow, reap, eat, sleep, and be merry.'

'But to be serious,' said Jack, assuming a grave expression of countenance, 'we are really in rather an uncomfortable position. If this is a desert island, we shall have to live very much like the wild beasts, for we have not a tool of any kind, not even a knife.'

'Yes, we have *that*,' said Peterkin, fumbling in his trousers pocket, from which he drew forth a small penknife with only one blade, and that was broken.

'Well, that's better than nothing; but come,' said Jack, rising, 'we are wasting our time in *talking* instead of *doing*. You seem well enough to walk now, Ralph. Let us see what we have got in our pockets, and then let us climb some hill and ascertain what sort of island we have been cast upon, for, whether good or bad, it seems likely to be our home for some time to come.'

We seated ourselves upon a rock and began to examine our property. When we reached the shore, after being wrecked, my companions had taken off part of their clothes and spread them out in the sun to dry, for, although the gale was raging fiercely, there was not a single cloud in the bright sky. They had also stripped off most of my wet clothes and spread them also on the rocks. Having resumed our garments, we now searched our pockets with the utmost care, and laid their contents out on a flat stone before us; and it was with no little anxiety that we turned our several pockets inside out, in order that nothing might escape us. We found that our worldly goods consisted of the following articles:

First, a small penknife with a single blade broken off about the middle and very rusty, besides having two or three notches on its edge. (Peterkin said of this, with his usual pleasantry, that it would do for a saw as well as a knife, which was a great advantage.) Second, an old German-silver pencil-case without any lead in it. Third, a piece of whip-cord about six yards long. Fourth, a sailmaker's needle of a small size. Fifth, a ship's telescope, which I happened to have in my hand at the time the ship struck, and which I clung to firmly all the time I was in the water. Indeed it was with difficulty that Jack got it out of my grasp when I was lying insensible on the shore. We did not see that it could be of much use to us, as the glass at the small end was broken to pieces. Our sixth article was a brass ring which Jack always wore on his little finger. I never understood why he wore it. Peterkin said 'it was in memory of the girl he left behind him!' In addition to these articles we had a little bit of tinder, and the clothes on our backs. These last were as follows:

Each of us had on a pair of stout canvas trousers, and a pair of sailors' thick shoes. Jack wore a red flannel shirt, a blue jacket, and a red Kilmarnock bonnet or night-cap, besides a pair of worsted socks, and a cotton pocket-hand-kerchief, with sixteen portraits of Lord Nelson printed on it, and a Union Jack in the middle. Peterkin had on a striped flannel shirt – which he wore outside his trousers, and belted round his waist, after the manner of a tunic – and a round black straw hat. Peterkin had also a pair of white cotton socks, and a blue handkerchief with white spots all over it. My own costume consisted of a blue flannel shirt, a blue jacket, a black cap, and a pair of worsted socks, besides the shoes and canvas trousers already mentioned. This was all we had, but we felt very thankful that we were possessed of so much.

While we were examining these things, and talking about them, Jack suddenly started and exclaimed: 'The oar! We have forgotten the oar.'

'What good will that do us?' said Peterkin. 'There's wood enough on the island to make a thousand oars.'

'Ay, lad,' replied Jack, 'but there's a bit of hoop iron at the end of it, and that may be of much use to us.'

'Very true,' said I, 'let us go fetch it'; and with that we all three rose and hastened down to the beach. I still felt a little weak from loss of blood, so that my companions soon began to leave me behind; but Jack perceived this, and turned back to help me. This was the first time that I had looked well about me since landing, as the spot where I had been laid was covered with thick bushes which almost hid the country from our view. As we now emerged from among these and walked down the sandy beach together, I cast my eyes about, and my spirits rose at the beautiful prospect which I beheld on every side. The gale had suddenly died away. The island on which we stood was hilly, and covered almost everywhere with the most beautiful and richly coloured trees, bushes, and shrubs, none of which I knew the names of at that time, except, indeed, the coconut palms, which I recognized at once from the many pictures that I had seen of them. A sandy beach of dazzling whiteness lined this bright green shore, and upon it there fell a gentle ripple of the sea. This last astonished me much, for at home the sea used to fall in huge billows on the shore long after a storm had subsided. But on casting my glance out to sea the cause became apparent. About a mile distant from the shore I saw the great billows of the ocean rolling like a green wall, and falling with a long, loud roar, upon a low coral reef, where they were dashed into white foam and flung up in clouds of spray. This spray sometimes flew exceedingly high, and, every here and there, a beautiful rainbow was formed for a moment among the falling drops. We afterwards found that this coral reef extended quite round the island, and formed a natural breakwater to it. Beyond this the sea rose and tossed violently from the effects of the storm; but between the reef and the shore it was as calm and as smooth as a pond.

My heart was filled with more delight than I can express at sight of so many glorious objects. I observed from the expression of my companion's countenance that he too derived much joy from the splendid scenery. The breeze was delightfully mild: and, when a puff blew off the land, it came laden with the most exquisite perfume that can be imagined. While we gazed, we were startled by a loud 'Huzza!' from Peterkin, and, on looking towards the edge of the sea, we saw him capering and jumping about like a monkey, and ever and anon tugging with all his might at something that lay upon the shore.

'What an odd fellow he is, to be sure,' said Jack, taking me by the arm and hurrying forward.

'Here it is, boys, hurrah! Come along. Just what we want,' cried Peterkin, as we drew near, still tugging with all his power.

On coming up we found that Peterkin was vainly endeavouring to pull the axe out of the oar, into which, it will be remembered, Jack struck it while endeavouring to cut away the cordage among which it had become entangled at the bow of the ship. Fortunately for us the axe had remained fast in the oar.

'Ah! that is capital indeed,' cried Jack, at the same time giving the axe a wrench that plucked it out of the tough wood. 'How fortunate this is! It will be of more value to us than a hundred knives, and the edge is quite new and sharp.'

'I'll answer for the toughness of the handle at any rate,' cried Peterkin; 'my arms are nearly pulled out of the sockets. But see here, our luck is great. There is iron on the blade.' He pointed to a piece of hoop iron which had been nailed round the blade of the oar to prevent it from splitting.

This also was a fortunate discovery. Jack went down on his knees, and with the edge of the axe began carefully to force out the nails. But as they were firmly fixed in, and the operation blunted our axe, we carried the oar up with us to the place where we had left the rest of our things, intending to burn the wood away from the iron at a more convenient time.

'Now, lads,' said Jack, 'I propose that we should go to the tail of the island, where the ship struck, which is only a quarter of a mile off, and see if anything else has been thrown ashore. When we get back here it will be time to have our supper and prepare our beds.'

'Agreed!' cried Peterkin and I together, as, indeed, we would have agreed to any proposal that Jack made.

Now, as we hastened along the white beach, which shone so brightly in the rays of the setting sun that our eyes were quite dazzled by its glare, it suddenly came into Peterkin's head that we had nothing to eat except the wild berries which grew in profusion at our feet.

'What shall we do, Jack?' said he, with a rueful look. 'Perhaps they may be poisonous!'

'No fear,' replied Jack, confidently; 'I have observed that a few of them are not unlike some of the berries that grow wild on our own native hills. Besides, I saw one or two strange birds eating them just a few minutes ago, and what won't kill the birds won't kill us. But look up there, Peterkin,' continued Jack, pointing to the branched head of a coconut palm. 'There are nuts for us in all stages.'

'So there are!' cried Peterkin, who had been too much taken up with other things to notice anything so high above his head as the fruit of a palm tree. The nuts had scarcely been pointed out to him when he bounded up the tall stem of the tree like a squirrel, and, in a few minutes, returned with three nuts, each as large as a man's fist.

'You had better keep them till we return,' said Jack. 'Let us finish our work before eating.'

'So be it, captain, go ahead,' cried Peterkin, thrusting the nuts into his trousers pocket. 'In fact I don't want to eat just now, but I would give a good deal for a drink. Oh, that I could find a spring! But I don't see the smallest sign of one hereabouts. I say, Jack, how does it happen that you seem to be up to everything? You have told us the names of half a dozen trees already, and yet you say that you were never in the South Seas before.'

'I'm not up to *everything*, Peterkin, as you'll find out ere long,' replied Jack, with a smile; 'but I have been a great reader of books of travel and adventure all my life, and that has put me up to a good many things. You said you were thirsty just a minute ago; now, jump up that tree and bring down a coconut – not a ripe one, bring a green, unripe one.'

Peterkin looked surprised, but obeyed.

'Now, cut a hole in it with your penknife, and clap it to your mouth, old fellow,' said Jack.

Peterkin did as he was directed, and we both burst into uncontrollable laughter at the changes that instantly passed over his expressive countenance. No sooner had he put the nut to his mouth, and thrown back his head in order to catch what came out of it, than his eyes opened to twice their ordinary size with astonishment, while his throat moved vigorously in the act of swallowing. Then a look of intense delight overspread his face, except, indeed, the mouth, which, being firmly fixed to the hole in the nut, could not take part in the expression; but he endeavoured to make up for this by winking at us excessively with his right eye. At length he stopped, and, drawing a long breath, exclaimed, 'Nectar! perfect nectar! I say, Jack, you're the best fellow I ever met in my life. Only taste that!' said he, holding the nut to my mouth. I drank, and certainly I was much surprised at the delightful liquid that flowed copiously down my throat. It was extremely cool, and had a sweet taste, mingled with acid; in fact, it was the likest thing to lemonade I ever tasted, and was most grateful and refreshing. I handed the nut to Jack, who, after tasting it, said: 'Now, Peterkin, you unbeliever, I never saw or tasted a coconut in my life before, except those sold in shops at home; but I once read that the green nuts contain that stuff, and you see it is true!'

'And pray,' asked Peterkin, 'what sort of "stuff" does the ripe nut contain?'

'A hollow kernel,' answered Jack, 'with a liquid like milk in it; but it does not satisfy thirst so well as hunger. It is very wholesome food, I believe.'

'Meat and drink on the same tree!' cried Peterkin. 'Washing in the sea, lodging on the ground – and all for nothing!' He tossed his straw hat in the air, and ran along the beach hallooing like a madman with delight.

We had now come to the point of rocks on which the ship had struck, but did not find a single article, although we searched carefully among the coral rocks, which at this place jutted out so far as nearly to join the reef that encircled the island. Just as we were about to return, however, we saw something black floating in a little cove that had escaped our observation. Running forward, we drew it from the water, and found it to be a long thick leather boot, such as fishermen at home wear; and a few paces farther on we picked up its fellow. We at once recognized these as having belonged to our captain. My first thought on seeing them was that our captain had been drowned; but Jack soon put my mind more at rest by saying that if the captain had been drowned with the boots on, he would certainly have been washed ashore along with them, and that he had no doubt whatever he had kicked them off while in the sea, that he might swim more easily.

Peterkin immediately put them on, but they were so large that, as Jack said, they would have done for boots, trousers, and vest too. I also tried them, but they were much too large in the feet for me; so we handed them to Jack. They fitted his large limbs and feet as if they had been made for him. However Jack did not use them often, as they were extremely heavy.

It was beginning to grow dark when we returned to our encampment; so we employed the light that yet remained to us in cutting down a quantity of boughs and the broad leaves of a tree, of which none of us knew the name. With these we erected a sort of rustic bower, in which to pass the night. There was no absolute necessity for this, because the air of our island was so genial and balmy that we could have slept quite well without any shelter; but we were so little used to sleeping in the open air that we did not quite relish the idea of lying down without any covering over us: besides, our bower would shelter us from the night dews or rain, if any should fall. Having strewed the floor with leaves and dry grass, we thought of supper.

But it now occurred to us, for the first time, that we had no means of making a fire.

'Now, there's a fix! – What shall we do?' said Peterkin, while we both turned our eyes to Jack, to whom we always looked in our difficulties. Jack seemed perplexed.

'There are flints enough, no doubt, on the beach,' said he, 'but they are of no use at all without a steel. However, we must try.' So saying, he went to the beach, and soon returned with two flints. On one of these he placed the tinder, and endeavoured to ignite it; but it was with great difficulty that a very small spark was struck out of the flints, and the tinder, being a bad, hard piece, would not catch. He then tried the bit of hoop iron, which would not strike fire at all; and after that the back of the axe, with no better success. During all these trials Peterkin sat with his hands in his pockets, his face growing longer at each successive failure.

'Oh dear!' he sighed. 'I would not care a button for the cooking of our victuals – perhaps they don't need it – but it's so dismal to eat one's supper in the dark, and we have had such a capital day, that it's a pity to finish off in this glum style. Oh, I have it!' he cried, starting up. 'The spy-glass – the big glass at the end is a burning-glass!'

'You forget that we have no sun,' said I.

Peterkin was silent; he had quite overlooked the absence of the sun.

'Ah, boys, I've got it now!' exclaimed Jack, rising and

looked up into the bright sky, and snuffed the scented air, his eyes glistened with delight. Then he gazed slowly round, till, observing the calm sea through an opening in the bushes, he started suddenly up as if he had received an electric shock, uttered a vehement shout, flung off his garments, and, rushing over the white sands, plunged into the water. The cry awoke Jack, who rose on his elbow with a look of surprise, followed by a quiet smile on seeing Peterkin in the water. Then Jack bounded to his feet, threw off his clothes, shook back his hair, and, with a lion-like spring, dashed over the sands and plunged into the sea with such force as quite to envelop Peterkin in a shower of spray. Jack was a remarkably good swimmer and diver, so that after his plunge we saw no sign of him for nearly a minute; after which he suddenly emerged, with a cry of joy, a good many yards out from the shore. I, too, hastily threw off my garments, and endeavoured to imitate Jack's vigorous bound; but I was so awkward that my foot caught on a stump, and I fell to the ground. However, when I got into the water I managed very well, for I was really a good swimmer, and diver too. I could not, indeed, equal Jack, who was superior to any Englishman I ever saw, but I infinitely surpassed Peterkin, who could only swim a little, and could not dive at all.

While Peterkin enjoyed himself in the shallow water, Jack and I swam out into the deep water, and occasionally dived for stones. I shall never forget my surprise and delight on first beholding the bottom of the sea. The water within the reef was as calm as a pond, and quite clear, from the surface to the bottom, so that we could see down easily even at a depth of twenty or thirty yards. When Jack and I dived in shallower water, we expected to have found sand and stones, instead of which we found ourselves in what appeared really to be an enchanted garden. The whole of the bottom of the lagoon, as we called the calm water within the reef, was covered with coral of every shape, size, and hue. Some portions were formed like large mushrooms; others appeared like the brain of a man; but the most common kind was a species of branching coral, and some portions were of a lovely pale pink colour, others pure white. Among this there grew large quantities of seaweed of the richest hues imaginable, and of the most graceful forms; while innumerable fishes – blue, red, yellow, green, and striped – sported in and out amongst the flower-beds of this submarine garden, and did not appear to be at all afraid of our approaching them.

On darting to the surface for breath, after our first dive, Jack and I rose close to each other.

'Did you ever in your life, Ralph, see anything so lovely?' said Jack.

'Never,' I replied. 'I can scarcely believe that we are not dreaming.'

'Dreaming!' cried Jack; 'do you know, Ralph, I'm half tempted to think that we really are dreaming. But if so I am resolved to make the most of it, and dream another dive; so here goes – down again, my boy!'

We took the second dive together, and I was greatly surprised to find that we could keep down much longer than in our own seas at home. I believe that this was owing to the heat of the water, which was so warm that we afterwards found we could remain in it for two and three hours at a time without feeling any unpleasant effects. When Jack reached the bottom, he grasped the coral stems, and crept along on his hands and knees, peeping under the seaweed and among the rocks. I observed him also pick up one or two large oysters, and retain them in his grasp, as if he meant to take them up with him, so I also gathered a few. Suddenly he made a grasp at a fish with blue and yellow stripes on its back, and actually touched its tail, but did not catch it. At this he turned towards me and attempted to smile; but no sooner had he done so than he sprang like an arrow to the surface, where, on following him, I found him gasping and coughing, and spitting water from his mouth. In a few minutes he recovered, and we both turned to swim ashore.

'I declare, Ralph,' said he, 'that I actually tried to laugh under water.'

'So I saw,' I replied; 'and I observed that you very nearly caught that fish by the tail. It would have done capitally for breakfast if you had.'

'Breakfast enough here,' said he, holding up the oysters, as we landed and ran up the beach. 'Hallo! Peterkin, here you are, boy. Split open these fellows while Ralph and I put on our clothes.'

Peterkin, who was already dressed, took the oysters, and opened them with the edge of our axe, exclaiming: 'Now, that *is* capital. There's nothing I'm so fond of.'

'Ah! that's lucky,' remarked Jack. 'I'll be able to keep you in good order now, Master Peterkin. You know you can't dive any better than a cat. So, sir, whenever you behave ill, you shall have no oysters for breakfast.'

'I'm very glad that our prospect of breakfast is so good,' said I, 'for I'm very hungry.'

'Here, then, stop your mouth with that, Ralph,' said Peterkin, holding a large oyster to my lips. I opened my mouth and swallowed it in silence, and it was remarkably good.

We now set ourselves earnestly about our preparations for spending the day. We had no difficulty with the fire this morning, as our burning-glass was an admirable one; and while we roasted a few oysters and ate our coconuts, we held a long, animated conversation about our plans for the future.

Our first care, after breakfast, was to place the few articles we possessed in the crevice of a rock at the farther end of a small cave which we discovered near our encampment. This cave, we hoped, might be useful to us as a store-house. Then we cut two large clubs off a species of very hard tree which grew near at hand. One of these was given to Peterkin, the other to me, and Jack armed himself with the axe. We took these precautions because we purposed to make an excursion to the top of the mountains of the interior, in order to obtain a better view of our island. Of course we knew not what dangers might befall us by the way, so thought it best to be prepared.

Having completed our arrangements and carefully extinguished our fire, we walked a short distance along the sea-beach, till we came to the entrance of a valley, through which flowed the rivulet before mentioned. Here we turned our backs on the sea and struck into the interior.

The prospect on entering the valley was truly splendid. On either side of us there was a gentle rise in the land, which thus formed two ridges about a mile apart on each side of the valley. These ridges – which, as well as the low grounds between them, were covered with trees and shrubs of the most luxuriant kind – continued to recede inland for about two miles, when they joined the foot of a small mountain. This hill rose rather abruptly from the head of the valley, and was entirely covered with trees, except on one particular spot near the left shoulder, where was a bare and rocky place of a broken and savage character. Beyond this hill we could not see, and we therefore directed our course up the banks of the rivulet towards the foot of it, intending to climb to the top.

Jack took the lead, carrying the axe on his shoulder. Peterkin, with his enormous club, came second. I brought up the rear, but, having been more taken up with the wonderful and curious things I saw at starting than with thoughts of possible danger, I had very foolishly left my club behind me. Although the trees and bushes were very luxuriant, they were not so thickly crowded together as to hinder our progress among them. We were able to wind in and out, and to follow the banks of the stream quite easily, although the height and thickness of the foliage prevented us from seeing far ahead. But sometimes a jutting-out rock on the hillsides afforded us a position whence we could enjoy the romantic view and mark our progress towards the foot of the hill. I was particularly struck, during the walk, with the richness of the undergrowth in most places, and recognized many berries and plants that resembled those of my native land. There were several kinds of flowers, too, but I did not see so many of these as I should have expected in such a climate. We also saw a great variety of small birds of bright plumage, and many parakeets similar to the one that awoke Peterkin so rudely in the morning.

We advanced to the foot of the hill without encountering anything to alarm us, except, indeed, once, when we were passing close under a part of the hill which was hidden from our view by the broad leaves of the banana trees, which grew in great luxuriance in that part. Jack was just preparing to force his way through this thicket, when we were startled and arrested by a strange pattering or rumbling sound.

'Hallo!' cried Peterkin, stopping short and grasping his club with both hands. 'What's that?'

Neither of us replied; but Jack seized his axe in his right hand, while with the other he pushed aside the broad leaves and endeavoured to peer amongst them.

'I can see nothing,' he said, after a short pause. 'I think it –'

Again the rumbling sound came, louder than before, and we all sprang back and stood on the defensive. For myself, having forgotten my club, I buttoned my jacket, doubled my fists, and threw myself into a boxing attitude. I must say, however, that I felt somewhat uneasy. Suddenly the pattering noise increased with tenfold violence. It was followed by a fearful crash among the bushes, which was rapidly repeated, as if some gigantic animal were bounding towards us. In another moment an enormous rock came crashing through the shrubbery, followed by a cloud of dust and small stones, and flew close past the spot where we stood, carrying bushes and young trees along with it.

'Pooh! Is that all?' exclaimed Peterkin, wiping the perspiration off his forehead. 'Why, I thought it was all the wild men and beasts in the South Sea Islands galloping on in one grand charge to sweep us off the face of the earth, instead of a mere stone tumbling down the mountain side.'

'Nevertheless,' remarked Jack, 'if that same stone had hit any of us, it would have rendered the charge you speak of quite unnecessary, Peterkin.'

On examining the spot more narrowly, we found that it lay

close to the foot of a very rugged precipice, from which stones of various sizes were always tumbling at intervals.

We now resumed our journey, resolving that in future we would be careful to avoid this dangerous precipice.

Soon afterwards we arrived at the foot of the hill and prepared to ascend it. Here Jack made a discovery which caused us all very great joy. This was a tree of a remarkably beautiful appearance, which Jack confidently declared to be the celebrated bread-fruit tree.

'Is it celebrated?' inquired Peterkin.

'It is,' replied Jack.

'That's odd, now,' rejoined Peterkin; 'I never heard of it before.'

'Then it's not so celebrated as I thought it was,' returned Jack, quietly squeezing Peterkin's hat over his eyes; 'but listen, you ignorant boobie, and hear of it now!'

Peterkin readjusted his hat, while Jack told us that this tree is one of the most valuable in the islands of the south; that it bears two, sometimes three, crops of fruit in the year; that the fruit is very like wheaten bread in appearance, and that it constitutes the principal food of many of the islanders.

'So,' said Peterkin, 'we seem to have everything in this wonderful island – lemonade ready bottled in nuts, and loaf-bread growing on the trees!'

Peterkin, as usual, was jesting; nevertheless, it is a curious fact that he spoke almost the literal truth.

'Moreover,' continued Jack, 'the bread-fruit tree affords a capital gum, which serves the natives for pitching their canoes; the bark of the young branches is made by them into cloth; and of the wood, which is durable and of a good colour, they build their houses. So you see, lads, that we have no lack of material here to make us comfortable.'

'But are you sure that that's it?' asked Peterkin.

'Quite sure,' replied Jack; 'for I was particularly interested in the account I once read of it, and I remember the description well. I am sorry, however, that I have forgotten the descriptions of many other trees which I am sure we have

31

seen today, if we could but recognize them. So, Peterkin, I'm not up to everything yet.'

'Never mind, Jack,' said Peterkin, patting his tall companion on the shoulder, 'never mind, Jack; you know a good deal for your age. You're a clever boy, sir; and if you only go on as you have begun, sir, you will –'

The end of this speech was suddenly cut short by Jack tripping up Peterkin's heels and tumbling him into a mass of thick shrubs, where, finding himself comfortable, he lay still, basking in the sunshine, while Jack and I examined the bread-fruit tree.

We were much struck with the deep, rich green colour of its broad leaves, which were twelve or eighteen inches long, deeply indented, and of a glossy smoothness like the laurel. The fruit, with which it was loaded, was nearly round, and about six inches in diameter, with a rough rind, marked with lozenge-shaped divisions. It was of various colours, from light pea-green to brown and rich yellow. Jack said that the yellow was the ripe fruit. The bark of the tree was rough and light-coloured; the trunk was about two feet in diameter, and it appeared to be twenty feet high, being quite destitute of branches up to that height, where it branched off into a beautiful and umbrageous head. The fruit hung in clusters of twos and threes on the branches; but as we were anxious to get to the top of the hill, we refrained from attempting to pluck any at that time.

Our hearts were now very much cheered by our good fortune, and it was with light and active steps that we clambered up the steep sides of the hill. On reaching the summit, a new and grander prospect met our gaze. We found that this was not the highest part of the island, but that another hill lay beyond, with a wide valley between it and the one on which we stood. This valley, like the first, was also full of rich trees. The beautiful blossoms on many of them threw a sort of rainbow tint over all, and gave to the valley the appearance of a garden of flowers. Among these we recognized many of the bread-fruit trees, laden with yellow fruit, and also a great many coconut palms. We pushed down the hillside, crossed the valley, and soon began to ascend the second mountain. It was clothed with trees nearly to the top, but the summit was bare, and in some places broken.

While on our way up we came to an object which filled us with much interest. This was the stump of a tree that had evidently been cut down with an axe! So we were not the first who had viewed this beautiful isle. The hand of man had been at work there before us. Perhaps the island was inhabited, although we had not seen any traces of man until now; but a second glance at the stump convinced us that we had not more reason to think so now than formerly; for the surface of the wood was quite decayed, and partly covered with fungus and green matter, so that it must have been cut many years ago.

'Perhaps,' said Peterkin, 'some ship or other has touched here long ago for wood, and only taken one tree.'

We did not think this likely, however, because, in such circumstances, the crew of a ship would cut wood of small size, and near the shore, whereas this was a large tree and stood near the top of the mountain. In fact it was the highest large tree on the mountain, all above it being wood of very recent growth.

'I can't understand it,' said Jack, scratching the surface of the stump with his axe. 'I can only suppose that the natives have been here and cut it for some purpose known only to themselves. But, hallo! What have we here?'

As he spoke, Jack began carefully to scrape away the moss and fungus from the stump, and soon laid bare three distinct traces of marks, as if some inscription or initials had been cut thereon. But although the traces were distinct, the exact form of the letters could not be made out. Jack thought they looked like J. S. but we could not be certain. Long exposure to the weather had so broken them up that we could not make out what they were. We were exceedingly perplexed at this discovery, and stayed a long time conjecturing what these marks could have been, but without avail; so, as the day was advancing, we quickly reached the top of the mountain.

We found this to be the highest point of the island, and from it we saw our kingdom lying, as it were, like a map around us. Our island consisted of two mountains. Between these lay a rich, beautiful valley. This valley crossed the island from one end to the other, being high in the middle and sloping on each side towards the sea. The large mountain sloped, on the side farthest from where we had been wrecked, gradually towards the sea; but a more careful observation showed that it was broken up into a multitude of very small dells and glens, intermingled with little rugged spots and small but abrupt precipices here and there, with rivulets tumbling over their edges and wandering down the slopes in little white streams. At the base of this mountain lay a narrow bright green plain which terminated abruptly at the shore. On the other side of the island, whence we had come, stood the smaller hill, at the foot of which diverged three valleys: one being that which we had ascended, with a smaller vale on each side of it, and separated from it by the two ridges before mentioned.

The diameter of the island seemed to be about ten miles. The entire island was belted by a beach of pure white sand. We now also observed that the coral reef completely encircled the island; but it varied its distance from it here and there, in some places being a mile from the beach, in others a few hundred yards, but the average distance was half a mile. The reef lay very low, and the spray of the surf broke over it in many places. This surf never ceased its roar, for, however calm the weather might be, there is always a gentle swaying motion in the great Pacific. The water within the lagoon was perfectly still. There were three narrow openings in the reef: one opposite each end of the valley which I have described as crossing the island; the other opposite our own valley, which we afterwards named the Valley of the Wreck. At each of these openings the reef rose into two small green islets, covered with bushes and having one or two coconut palms on each. These islets were very singular, and appeared as if planted expressly for the purpose of marking the channel into the lagoon. Our captain was making for one of these openings the day we were wrecked, and would have reached it too had not the rudder been torn away. Within the lagoon were several pretty, low coral islands, just opposite our encampment; and, immediately beyond these, out at sea, lay about a dozen other islands, at various distances, from half a mile to ten miles, all of them smaller than ours and apparently uninhabited.

All this we noted, and a great deal more, while we sat on the top of the mountain. After we had satisfied ourselves we prepared to return; but here again we discovered traces of the presence of man. These were a pole or staff and one or two pieces of wood which had been squared with an axe. All of these were, however, very much decayed, and they had evidently not been touched for many years.

Full of these discoveries we returned to our encampment. On the way we fell in with the traces of some four-footed animal. This also tended to raise our hopes of obtaining some animal food on the island, so we reached home in good spirits, quite prepared for supper, and highly satisfied with our excursion.

CHAPTER IV

For several days we did not wander far from our encampment, but gave ourselves up to forming plans for the future and making our present abode comfortable.

There were various causes for this comparative inaction. In the first place, although everything around us was so delightful, we did not quite like the idea of settling down here for the rest of our lives. Then there was a little uncertainty still as to there being natives on the island, and we entertained a faint hope that a ship might come and take us off. But as day after day passed we gave up all hope of an early deliverance and set diligently to work at our homestead.

During this time, however, we had not been altogether idle. We made several experiments in cooking the coconut, most of which did not improve it. Then we removed our goods, and took up our abode in the cave, but found the change so bad that we returned gladly to the bower. Besides this, we bathed very frequently, and talked a great deal. Among other useful things, Jack converted about three inches of the hoop iron into an excellent knife. First he beat it quite flat with the axe. Then he made a rude handle, and tied the hoop iron to it with our piece of whip-cord, and ground it to an edge on a piece of sandstone. When it was finished he used it to shape a better handle, to which he fixed it with a strip of his cotton handkerchief – in which operation he had, as Peterkin pointed out, torn off one of Lord Nelson's noses. However, the whip-cord, thus set free, was used by Peterkin as a fishing line. He merely tied a piece of oyster to the end of it. This the fish were allowed to swallow, and then they were pulled quickly ashore. But as the line was very short and we had no boat, the fish we caught were exceedingly small.

One day Peterkin came up from the beach, where he had been angling, and said in a very cross tone: 'I'll tell you what, Jack, I'm not going to catch such contemptible things any longer. I want you to swim out with me on your back, and let me fish in deep water!'

'Dear me, Peterkin,' replied Jack, 'I had no idea you were taking the thing so much to heart. Let me see' – and Jack looked down at a piece of timber on which he had been labouring, with a peculiar gaze of abstraction, which he always assumed when trying to invent or discover anything.

'What say you to building a boat?' he inquired.

'Take far too long,' was the reply; 'can't be bothered waiting. I want to begin at once!'

Again Jack considered. 'I have it!' he cried. 'We'll fell a large tree and launch the trunk of it in the water, so that when you want to fish you've nothing to do but to swim out to it.'

'Would not a small raft do better?' said I.

'Much better; but we have no ropes to bind it together with. Perhaps we may find something hereafter that will do as well, but, in the meantime, let us try the tree.'

This was agreed on, so we started off to a spot where we knew of a tree that would suit us, which grew near the water's edge. As soon as we reached it Jack threw off his coat, and, wielding the axe with his sturdy arms, hacked and hewed at it for a quarter of an hour without stopping. Then he paused, and, while he sat down to rest, I continued the work. Then Peterkin made a vigorous attack on it, so that when Jack renewed his powerful blows, a few minutes' cutting brought it down with a crash.

'Hurrah! now for it,' cried Jack; 'off with its head.'

So saying he began to cut through the stem again, at about six yards from the thick end. This done, he cut three strong, short poles or levers from the stout branches, with which to roll the log down the beach; for, as it was nearly two feet thick at the large end, we could not move it without such helps. With the levers, however, we rolled it slowly into the sea.

Having been thus successful in launching our vessel, we

next shaped the levers into rude oars or paddles, and then attempted to embark. This was easy enough to do; but, after seating ourselves astride the log, it was with the utmost difficulty we kept it from rolling round and plunging us into the water. Not that we minded that much; but we preferred, if possible, to fish in dry clothes. To be sure, our trousers were necessarily wet, as our legs were dangling in the water on each side of the log; but, as they could be easily dried, we did not care. After half an hour's practice, we became expert enough to keep our balance pretty steadily. Then Peterkin laid down his paddle, and having baited his line with a whole oyster, dropped it into deep water.

'Now, then, Jack,' said he, 'be cautious; steer clear o' that seaweed. There; that's it; gently, now, gently. I see a fellow at least a foot long down there, coming to – ha! that's it! Oh! bother, he's off.'

'Did he bite?' said Jack, urging the log onwards a little with his paddle.

'Bite? Ay! He took it into his mouth, but the moment I began to haul he opened his jaws and let it out again.'

'Let him swallow it next time,' said Jack, laughing.

'There he is again,' cried Peterkin, his eyes flashing with excitement. 'Look out! Now then! No! Yes! No! Why, the brute *won't* swallow it!'

'Try to haul him up by the mouth, then,' cried Jack. 'Do it gently.'

A heavy sigh and a look of blank despair showed that poor Peterkin had tried and failed again.

'Never mind, lad,' said Jack, in a voice of sympathy; 'we'll move on, and offer it to some other fish.' So saying, Jack plied his paddle, but scarcely had he moved from the spot, when a fish with an enormous head and a little body darted from under a rock and swallowed the bait at once.

'Got him this time – that's a fact!' cried Peterkin, hauling in the line. 'He's swallowed the bait right down to his tail, I declare. Oh, what a thumper!'

As the fish came struggling to the surface, we leaned

forward to see it, and overbalanced the log. Peterkin threw his arms round the fish's neck; and, in another instant, we were all floundering in the water!

A shout of laughter burst from us as we rose to the surface like three drowned rats, and seized hold of the log. We soon recovered our position, and sat more warily, while Peterkin secured the fish, which had well-nigh escaped in the midst of our struggles. It was little worth having, however; but, as Peterkin remarked, it was better than the smouts he had been catching for the last two or three days; so we laid it on the log before us, and having re-baited the line, dropped it in again for another.

Now, while we were thus intent upon our sport, our attention was suddenly attracted by a ripple on the sea, just a few yards away from us. Peterkin shouted to us to paddle in that direction, as he thought it was a big fish, and we might have a chance of catching it. But Jack, instead of complying, said, in a deep, earnest tone of voice, which I never before heard him use: 'Haul up your line, Peterkin; seize your paddle; quick – it's a shark!'

The horror with which we heard this may well be imagined, for our legs were hanging down in the water, and we could not pull them up without upsetting the log. Peterkin instantly hauled up the line; and, grasping his paddle, exerted himself to the utmost, while we also did our best to make for shore. But we were a good way off, and the log being very heavy, moved but slowly through the water. We now saw the shark quite distinctly swimming round and round us, its sharp fin every now and then protruding above the water. Jack urged us vehemently to paddle for our lives, while he himself set us the example. Suddenly he shouted, 'Look out! – there he comes!' and in a second we saw the monstrous fish dive close under us, and turn half over on his side. But we all made a great commotion with our paddles, which no doubt frightened it away for that time, as we saw it immediately after circling round us as before.

'Throw the fish to him,' cried Jack, in a quick, suppressed

voice; 'we'll make the shore in time yet if we can keep him off for a few minutes.'

Peterkin stopped one instant to obey the command, and then plied his paddle again with all his might. No sooner had the fish fallen on the water than we observed the shark sink. In another second we saw its white breast rising; for sharks always turn over on their sides when about to seize their prey, their mouths being not at the point of their heads like those of other fish, but under their chins. In another moment his snout rose above the water – his wide jaws, armed with a terrific double row of teeth, appeared. The dead fish was engulfed, and the shark sank out of sight. But Jack was mistaken in supposing that it would be satisfied. In a very few minutes it returned, and its quick motions led us to fear that it would attack us at once.

'Stop paddling,' cried Jack, suddenly. 'I see it coming up behind us. Now, obey my orders *quickly*. Our lives may depend on it. Ralph, Peterkin, do your best to *balance the log*. Don't look out for the shark. Don't glance behind you. Do nothing but balance the log.'

Peterkin and I instantly did as we were ordered, for we had implicit confidence in Jack's courage and wisdom. For a few seconds we sat thus silently; but I could not resist glancing backward. On doing so, I saw Jack sitting rigid like a statue, with his paddle raised, his lips compressed, and his eyebrows bent over his eyes, which glared savagely down into the water. I also saw the shark, to my horror, quite close under the log, in the act of darting towards Jack's foot. I could scarce suppress a cry on beholding this. In another moment the shark rose. Jack drew his leg suddenly from the water, and threw it over the log. The monster's snout rubbed against the log as it passed, and revealed its hideous jaws, into which Jack instantly plunged the paddle, and thrust it down its throat. So violent was this act that Jack rose to his feet in performing it; the log was thereby rolled completely over, and we were once more plunged into the water. We all rose, spluttering and gasping, in a moment.

'Now, then, strike out for shore,' cried Jack. 'Here, Peterkin, catch hold of my collar, and kick out with a will.'

Peterkin did as he was desired, and Jack cut through the water like a boat; while I, being free from all encumbrance, succeeded in keeping up with him. A few minutes more sufficed to carry us into shallow water; and, finally, we landed in safety, though very much exhausted.

Our encounter with the shark was the first great danger that had befallen us since landing on this island, and we felt very seriously affected by it, especially when we considered that we had so often unwittingly incurred the same danger while bathing. We were now forced to take to fishing in the shallow water, until we could construct a raft. What troubled us most, however, as that we were compelled to forgo our morning swimming excursions. We did, indeed, continue to enjoy our bathe in the shallow water, but Jack and I found that one great source of our enjoyment was gone, when we could no longer dive down among the beautiful coral groves at the bottom of the lagoon. We had come to be so fond of this exercise, and to take such an interest in watching the formations of coral and the gambols of the many beautiful fish amongst the forests of red and green seaweeds, that we had become quite familiar with the appearance of the fish and the localities that they chiefly haunted. We had also become expert divers. But we made it a rule never to stay long under water at a time. Jack told me that to do so often was bad for the lungs.

Sometimes, when Jack happened to be in a humorous frame, he would seat himself at the bottom of the sea on one of the brain corals, and then make faces at me, in order to make me laugh under water. At first, when he took me unawares, he nearly succeeded, and I had to shoot to the surface in order to laugh; but afterwards I became aware of his intentions, and had no difficulty in restraining myself. Peterkin would have liked to be with us; and he often expressed much regret at being unable to join us. So one day we prevailed on him to try to go down with us. But Peterkin was very nervous in the water, and it was with difficulty we got him to consent to be taken down. But no sooner had we pulled him down a yard or so into the deep clear water, than he began to struggle and kick violently, so we were forced to let him go, when he rose out of the water like a cork, gave a loud gasp and a frightful roar, and struck out for the land with the utmost possible haste.

Now, all this pleasure we were to forgo, and Jack and I felt very much depressed. Our difficulty induced us to think of searching for a large pool among the rocks, where the water should be deep enough for diving, yet so surrounded by rocks as to prevent sharks from getting at us. And such a pool we afterwards found. It was not more than ten minutes' walk from our camp, and was in the form of a small deep bay or basin, the entrance to which, besides being narrow, was so shallow that no fish so large as a shark could get in, at least not unless he should be a remarkably thin one.

Inside the basin, which we called our Water Garden, the coral formations were much more wonderful, and the sea-weed plants far more vividly coloured, than in the lagoon itself. And the water was so clear and still that, although very deep, you could see the minutest object at the bottom. Besides this, there was a ledge of rock which overhung the basin at its deepest part, from which we could dive pleasantly, and whereon Peterkin could sit and see not only all the wonders I had described to him, but also Jack and me creeping amongst the marine shrubbery at the bottom, like – as he expressed it – 'two great white sea-monsters'. During these excursions of ours to the bottom of the sea, we began to get an insight into the manners and customs of its inhabitants, and to make discoveries of wonderful things. Among other things, we were deeply interested with the operations of the little coral insect which, I was informed by Jack, is supposed to have entirely constructed many of the numerous islands in the Pacific Ocean.

I also became much taken up with the manners and

appearance of the anemones, and starfish, and crabs, and sea-urchins, and suchlike creatures; and was not content with watching those I saw during my dives in the Water Garden, but I must needs scoop out a hole in the coral rock close to it, which I filled with salt water, and stocked with anemones and shell-fish, in order to watch more closely how they were in the habit of passing their time. Our burning-glass also now became a great treasure to me, as it enabled me to magnify, and so to perceive more clearly these curious creatures of the deep.

Having now got ourselves into a very comfortable condition, we began to talk of a project which we had long had in contemplation – namely, to travel entirely round the island, in order to see whether there might be any place more convenient and suitable for our permanent residence. Not that we were in any degree dissatisfied with it; on the contrary, we entertained quite a home-feeling to our bower and its neighbourhood; but if a better place did exist, there was no reason why we should not make use of it.

We had much earnest talk over this matter. But Jack proposed that, before undertaking such an excursion, we should supply ourselves with good defensive arms, for, as we intended not only to go round all the shore, but to ascend most of the valleys, we should be likely to meet, he would not say *dangers*, but at least with everything that existed on the island, whatever that might be.

'Besides,' said Jack, 'it won't do for us to live on coconuts and oysters always. No doubt they are very excellent in their way, but I think a little animal food now and then would be good for us; and as there are many small birds among the trees, some of which are probably very good to eat, I think it would be a capital plan to make bows and arrows, with which we could easily knock them over.'

'First rate!' cried Peterkin. 'You will make the bows, Jack, and I'll try my hand at the arrows. The fact is, I'm quite tired of throwing stones at the birds. I began the very day we landed, but I've never hit anything yet.'

'You forget,' said I, 'you hit me one day on the shin.'

'Ah, true,' replied Peterkin, 'and a precious shindy you kicked up in consequence. But you were at least four yards away from the impudent parakeet I aimed at; so you see what a horribly bad shot I am.'

'But,' said I, 'Jack, you cannot make three bows and arrows before tomorrow, and would it not be a pity to waste time, now that we have made up our minds to go on this expedition? Suppose that you make one bow and arrow for yourself, and we can take our clubs?'

'That's true, Ralph. The day is pretty far advanced, and I doubt if I can make even one bow before dark. To be sure I might work by fire-light, after the sun goes down.'

We had, up to this time, been in the habit of going to bed with the sun. Our work during the day was usually hard enough – what between fishing, and improving our bower, and diving in the Water Garden, and rambling in the woods; so that, when night came, we were usually very glad to retire to our beds. But now that we had a desire to work at night, we felt a wish for candles.

'Won't a good blazing fire give you light enough?' enquired Peterkin.

'Yes,' replied Jack, 'quite enough; but then it will give us a great deal more than enough of heat in this warm climate of ours. The fact is, I've been thinking over this subject before. There is a certain nut growing in these islands which is called the candle-nut, because the natives use it instead of candles, and I know all about it, and how to prepare it for burning –'

'Then why don't you do it?' interrupted Peterkin. 'Why have you kept us in the dark so long, you vile philosopher?'

'Because,' said Jack, 'I have not seen the tree yet, and I'm not sure that I should know either the tree or the nuts if I did see them. I believe the nut is about the size of a walnut; and I think that the leaves are white, but I am not sure.'

'Ha!' exclaimed Peterkin, 'I saw a tree answering to that description this very day.'

'Then lead me to it,' said Jack, seizing his axe.

We soon came to the tree in question, which, after Jack had closely examined it, we concluded must be the candle-nut tree. Its leaves were of a beautiful silvery white, and formed a fine contrast to the dark-green foliage of the surrounding trees. We immediately filled our pockets with the nuts, after which Jack said: 'Now, Peterkin, climb that coco-nut tree and cut me one of the long branches.'

This was soon done, but it cost some trouble, for the stem was very high. The leaf or branch was a very large one, and we were surprised at its size and strength. Viewed from a little distance, the coconut tree seems to be a tall, straight stem, without a single branch except at the top, where there is a tuft of feathery-looking leaves. But when we saw one of these leaves or branches at our feet, we found it to be a strong stalk, about fifteen feet long, with a number of narrow, pointed leaflets ranged alternately on each side. But what seemed to us the most wonderful thing about it was a curious substance resembling cloth, which was wrapped round the thick end of the stalk, where it had been cut from the tree. Peterkin told us that he had the greatest difficulty in separating the branch from the stem, on account of this substance, as it was wrapped quite round the tree and round all the other branches, thus forming a strong support to the large leaves while exposed to high winds. This cloth was remarkably like coarse brown cotton cloth. It had a seam or fibre down the centre of it, from which diverged other fibres, about the size of a bristle. There were two layers of these fibres, very long and tough, the one layer crossing the other obliquely, and the whole was cemented together with a still finer fibrous and adhesive substance. When we regarded it attentively, we could with difficulty believe that it had not been woven by human hands. This remarkable piece of cloth we stripped carefully off, and found it to be above two feet long, by a foot broad, and we carried it home with us as a great prize.

Jack now took one of the leaflets, and, cutting out the central spine or stalk, hurried back with it to our camp. Having made a small fire, he baked the nuts slightly, and then peeled off the husks. After this he wished to bore a hole in them, which he did with the point of our useless pencil-case. Then he strung them on the coconut spine, and on putting a light to the topmost nut, we found to our joy that it burned with a clear, beautiful flame; upon seeing which, Peterkin sprang up and danced round the fire for at least five minutes in the excess of his satisfaction.

'Now, lads,' said Jack, extinguishing our candle, 'the sun will set in an hour, so we have no time to lose. I shall go and cut a young tree to make my bow, and you had better go and select good strong sticks for clubs, and we'll set to work at them after dark.'

So saying he shouldered his axe and went off, followed by Peterkin, while I took up the piece of newly discovered cloth, and fell to examining its structure. So engrossed was I in this that I was still sitting in the same attitude and occupation when my companions returned.

'I told you so!' cried Peterkin, with a loud laugh. 'Oh, Ralph, you're incorrigible. See, there's a club for you. I was sure, when we left you looking at that bit of stuff, that we would find you poring over it when we came back, so I just cut a club for you as well as for myself.'

'Thank you, Peterkin,' said I.

As it was now getting dark we lighted our candle, and placing it in a holder made of two crossing branches, inside our bower, we seated ourselves on our leafy beds and began to work.

'I intend to appropriate the bow for my own use,' said Jack, chipping the piece of wood he had brought with his axe. 'I used to be a pretty fair shot once. But what's that you're doing?' he added, looking at Peterkin, who had drawn the end of a long pole into the tent, and was endeavouring to fit a small piece of the hoop iron to the end of it.

'I'm going to enlist into the Lancers,' answered Peterkin. 'You see, Jack, I find the club rather an unwieldy instrument for my delicately formed muscles, and I flatter myself I shall do more execution with a spear.'

'Well, if length constitutes power,' said Jack, 'you'll certainly be invincible.'

The pole which Peterkin had cut was full twelve-feet long, being a very strong but light and tough young tree, which merely required thinning at the butt to be a serviceable weapon.

'That's a very good idea,' said I. 'And, now I think of it, I'll change my plan too. I don't think much of a club, so I'll make me a sling out of this piece of cloth. I used to be very fond of slinging, ever since I read of David slaying Goliath, and I was once thought to be expert at it.'

So I set to work to manufacture a sling. For a long time we all worked very busily without speaking. While we were thus engaged, we were startled by a distant but most strange and horrible cry. It seemed to come from the sea. Rushing out of our bower, we hastened down to the beach and stayed to listen. Again it came quite loud and distinct on the night air – a prolonged, hideous cry, something like the braying of an ass. The moon had risen, and we could see the islands in and beyond the lagoon quite plainly, but there was no object visible to account for such a cry. A strong gust of wind was blowing from the point whence the sound came, but this died away while we were gazing out to sea.

'What can it be?' said Peterkin, in a low whisper, while we all involuntarily crept closer to each other.

'Do you know,' said Jack, 'I have heard that mysterious sound twice before, but never so loud as tonight.'

We listened for a long time for the sound again, but as it did not come, we returned to the bower.

'Very strange,' said Peterkin, quite gravely. 'Do you believe in ghosts, Ralph?'

'No,' I answered, 'I do not. Nevertheless I must confess that strange, unaccountable sounds, such as we have just heard, make me feel a little uneasy.'

'What say you to it, Jack?'

'I neither believe in ghosts nor feel uneasy,' he replied. 'I never saw a ghost myself, and I never met with anyone who

47

had. I certainly can't imagine what *that* sound is; but I'm quite sure I shall find out before long – and if it's a ghost I'll – I'll –'

'Eat it,' cried Peterkin.

'Yes, I'll eat it! Now, then, my bow and two arrows are finished; so if you're ready we had better turn in.'

By this time Peterkin had thinned down his spear and tied an iron point very cleverly to the end of it; I had formed a sling, the lines of which were composed of thin strips of the coconut cloth, plaited; and Jack had made a stout bow, nearly five feet long, with two arrows, feathered with two or three large plumes which some bird had dropped. They had no barbs, but Jack said that if arrows were well feathered, they did not require iron points, but would fly quite well if merely sharpened at the point.

'A feathered arrow without a barb,' said he, 'is a good weapon, but a barbed arrow without feathers is utterly useless.'

The string of the bow was formed of our piece of whipcord, part of which, as he did not like to cut it, was rolled round the bow.

We spent the whole of the next day in practising. And it was well we did so, for we found that our arms were very imperfect. First, Jack found that the bow was much too strong, and he had to thin it. Also the spear was much too heavy, and so had to be reduced in thickness, although nothing would induce Peterkin to have it shortened. My sling answered very well, but I had fallen so much out of practice that my first stone knocked off Peterkin's hat, and narrowly missed making a second Goliath of him. However, after having spent the whole day in diligent practice, we began to find some of our former expertness returning – at least Jack and I did. As for Peterkin, being naturally a neat-handed boy, he soon handled his spear well, and could run full tilt at a coconut, and hit it with great precision once out of every five times.

That night we examined and repaired our arms ere we lay

down to rest, although we were much fatigued, in order that we might be in readiness to set out at daylight on the following morning.

CHAPTER V

Scarcely had the sun shot its first ray across the broad Pacific, when Jack sprang to his feet, and hallooing in Peterkin's ear to awaken him, ran down the beach to take his customary dip in the sea. We did not bathe that morning in our Water Garden, but to save time refreshed ourselves in the shallow water just opposite the bower. Our breakfast was also dispatched without loss of time, and in less than an hour all our preparations for the journey were completed.

In addition to his ordinary dress, Jack tied a belt of coconut cloth round his waist, into which he thrust the axe. I was also advised to put on a belt and carry a short cudgel or bludgeon in it; for, as Jack remarked, the sling would be of little use if we should chance to come to close quarters with any wild animal. As for Peterkin, notwithstanding that he carried such a long spear over his shoulder, we could not prevail on him to leave his club behind; 'for', said he, 'a spear at close quarters is not worth a button.'

We did not consider it necessary to carry any food with us, as we knew that wherever we went we should be certain to fall in with coconut trees; having which, we were amply supplied, as Peterkin said, with meat and drink and pocket-handkerchiefs! I took the precaution, however, to put the burning-glass into my pocket, lest we should want fire.

The morning was exceedingly lovely. It was one of that very still and peaceful sort which made the few noises that we heard seem to be *quiet* noises. I know no other way of expressing this idea. Such sounds as I refer to were, the peculiarly melancholy plaint of sea-birds floating on the glassy water, or sailing in the sky, the faint ripples on the beach, and the solemn boom of the surf upon the distant coral reef. We felt very glad in our hearts as we walked along the sands. For my part, I felt so deeply overjoyed, that I was surprised at my own sensations. Peterkin's happiness was also very great; yet he did not express this by dancing as was his wont, but walked quietly between us with a joyful smile upon his countenance.

I have said that Peterkin walked along the sands between us. We had two ways of walking together about our island. When we travelled through the woods, we always did so in single file. In such cases Jack always took the lead, Peterkin followed, and I brought up the rear. But when we travelled along the sands, which extended almost in an unbroken line of glistening white round the island, we marched abreast, as we found this method more sociable.

We were now fairly started. For some time we advanced at a brisk pace without speaking. After passing the ridge of land that formed one side of our valley – the Valley of the Wreck – we beheld another small vale lying before us in all the luxuriant loveliness of tropical vegetation. We were about to explore this valley, when Peterkin stopped us, and directed our attention to a very remarkable appearance along the shore.

'What's yon, think you?' said he, levelling his spear, as if he expected an immediate attack from the object in question, though it was full half a mile distant.

As he spoke, there appeared a white column above the rocks, as if of steam or spray. It rose upwards to a height of several feet, and then disappeared. Had this been near the sea, we would not have been so greatly surprised, as it might in that case have been the surf. But this white column appeared about fifty yards inland. The rocks at the place were rugged, and they stretched across the sandy beach into the sea. Scarce had we ceased expressing our surprise at this sight, when another column flew upwards for a few seconds, not far from the spot where the first had been seen, and disappeared; and so, at long irregular intervals, these strange sights recurred. We were now quite sure that the columns were watery or composed of spray, but what caused them we could not guess.

In a few minutes we gained the spot, which was very rugged and precipitous, and quite damp with the falling of the spray. We had much ado to pass over dry-shod. The ground also was full of holes. Now, while we stood anxiously waiting for the reappearance of these water-spouts, we heard a low, rumbling sound near us, which quickly increased to a gurgling and hissing noise, and a moment afterwards a thick spout of water burst upwards from a hole in the rock, and spouted into the air with much violence, and so close to where Jack and I were standing that it nearly touched us. We sprang to one side, but not before a cloud of spray descended, and drenched us both to the skin.

Peterkin, who was standing farther off, escaped with a few drops, and burst into an uncontrollable fit of laughter on beholding our miserable plight.

'Mind your eye!' he shouted. 'There goes another!' The words were scarcely out of his mouth when there came up a spout from another hole, which served us exactly as before.

Peterkin now shrieked with laughter; but his merriment was abruptly put a stop to by the gurgling noise occurring close to where he stood.

'Where'll it spout this time, I wonder?' he said, preparing to run. Suddenly there came a loud hiss or snort; a fierce spout of water burst up between Peterkin's legs, blew him off his feet, enveloped him in its spray, and hurled him to the ground. He fell with so much violence that we feared he must have broken some of his bones, and ran anxiously to his assistance; but fortunately he had fallen on a clump of tangled herbage, in which he lay sprawling.

It was now our turn to laugh; but as we knew not when or where the next spout might arise, we assisted him hastily to jump up and hurry from the spot.

'What's to be done now?' enquired Peterkin, ruefully.

'Make a fire, lad, and dry ourselves,' replied Jack.

In about an hour after this mishap our clothes were again

dried. While they were hanging up before the fire, we walked down to the beach, and soon observed that these curious spouts took place immediately after the fall of a huge wave, never before it; and, moreover, that the spouts did not take place excepting when the billow was an extremely large one. From this we concluded that there must be a subterraneous channel in the rock into which the water was driven by the larger waves, and finding no way of escape except through these small holes, was thus forced up violently through them. At any rate, we could not conceive any other reason for these strange water-spouts.

'I say, Ralph, what's that in the water – is it a shark?' said Jack, just as we were about to quit the place.

I immediately ran to the overhanging ledge of rock, from which he was looking down into the sea, and bent over it. There I saw a very faint pale object of a greenish colour, which seemed to move slightly.

'It's like a fish of some sort,' said I.

'Hallo, Peterkin!' cried Jack. 'Fetch your spear; here's work for it.'

But when we tried to reach the object, the spear proved to be too short.

Jack now drove the spear forcibly towards the object, and let go his hold; but, although it seemed to be well aimed, he must have missed, for the handle soon rose again; and when the spear was drawn up, there was the pale green object in exactly the same spot, slowly moving its tail.

'Very odd,' said Jack.

But although it was undoubtedly very odd, and although Jack and all of us plunged the spear at it repeatedly, we could neither hit it nor drive it away, so we were compelled to continue our journey without discovering what it was.

Our examination of the little valley proved to be altogether most satisfactory. We found in it not only similar trees to those we had already seen in our own valley, but also one or two others of a different species. We had also the satisfaction of discovering a peculiar vegetable, which Jack concluded must certainly be that of which he had read and which was named *taro*. Also we found a large supply of yams, and another root like a potato in appearance. As these were all quite new to us, we regarded our lot as a most fortunate one, in being thus cast on an island so well stored with all the necessaries of life. We each put one of these roots in our pocket, intending to use them for our supper; of which more hereafter. We also saw many beautiful birds here, and traces of some four-footed animal again. Meanwhile the sun began to descend, so we returned to the shore, and pushed on round the spouting rocks into the next valley. This was that valley of which I have spoken as running across the entire island. It was by far the largest and most beautiful that we had yet looked upon. Here were trees of every shape and size and hue, many of which we had not seen in the other valleys; for, the stream in this valley being larger, and the mould much richer than in the Valley of the Wreck, it was clothed with a more luxuriant growth of trees and plants. Some trees were dark glossy green, others of a rich and warm hue, contrasting well with those of a pale light green, which were everywhere abundant. Among these we recognized the broad dark heads of the bread-fruit, with its golden fruit; the pure, silvery foliage of the candle-nut, and several species which bore a strong resemblance to the pine.

Now, while we were gazing in silent admiration, Jack uttered an exclamation of surprise, and, pointing to an object a little to one side of us, said: 'That's a banian tree.'

'And what's a banian tree?' enquired Peterkin, as we walked towards it.

'A very curious one, as you shall see presently,' replied Jack. 'It is called the *aoa* here, if I recollect rightly, and has a wonderful peculiarity about it. What an enormous one it is, to be sure.'

'*It!*' repeated Peterkin. 'Why, there are dozens of banians here!'

'There is but one tree here of this kind,' returned Jack, 'as you will perceive if you will examine it.' And, sure enough, what we had supposed was a forest of trees was in reality only one. Its bark was of a light colour, and had a shining appearance, the leaves being lance-shaped, small, and of a beautiful pea-green. But the wonderful thing about it was that the branches, which grew out from the stem horizontally, sent down long shoots or fibres to the ground, which, taking root, had themselves become trees, and were covered with bark like the tree itself. Many of these fibres had descended from the branches at various distances, and thus supported them on natural pillars, some of which were so large and strong that it was not easy at first to distinguish the offspring from the parent stem. The fibres were of all sizes and in all states of advancement, from pillars to small cords which hung down and were about to take root. In short, it seemed to us that, if there were only space afforded to it, this single tree would at length cover the whole island.

Shortly after this we came upon another remarkable tree, which merits description. It was a splendid chestnut, but its proper name Jack did not know. However, there were quantities of fine nuts upon it, some of which we put in our pockets. But its stem was the wonderful part of it. It rose to about twelve feet without a branch, and was not of great thickness; on the contrary, it was remarkably slender for the size of the tree; but, to make up for this, there were four or five wonderful projections in this stem. Suppose that five planks two inches thick and three feet broad had been placed round the trunk of the tree, with their *edges* closely fixed to it, from the ground up to the branches, and that these planks had been covered over with the bark of the tree and incorporated with it. In short, they were just natural buttresses, without which the stem could not have supported its heavy and umbrageous top. We found these chestnuts to be very numerous. They grew chiefly on the banks of the stream, and were of all sizes.

While we were examining a small tree of this kind, Jack clipped a piece off a buttress with his axe, and found the wood to be firm and easily cut. He then struck the axe into it with all his force, and very soon split it off close to the tree, first, however, having cut it across transversely above and below. By this means he satisfied himself that we could now obtain short planks, as it were already sawn, of any size and thickness that we desired: a very great discovery indeed, perhaps the most important we had yet made.

We now wended our way back to the coast, intending to encamp near the beach, as we found that the mosquitoes were troublesome in the forest. On our way we could not help admiring the birds which flew and chirped around us. Among them we observed a pretty kind of parakeet, with a green body, a blue head, and a red breast; also a few beautiful turtle-doves, and several flocks of wood-pigeons. The hues of many of these birds were extremely vivid – bright green, blue, and scarlet being the prevailing tints. As evening drew on a flock of pigeons flew past. I slung a stone into the midst of them at a venture, and had the good fortune to kill one. We were startled, soon after, by a loud whistling noise above our heads; and on looking up, saw a flock of wild ducks making for the coast. Observing where they alighted, we followed them up until we came upon a most lovely blue lake, not more than two hundred yards long, embosomed in verdant trees. Its placid surface was covered with various species of wild duck, feeding among the sedges and broad-leaved water-plants which floated on it, while numerous birds like water-hens ran to and fro most busily on its margin. These all flew tumultuously away the instant we made our appearance.

Now, as we neared the shore, Jack and I said we would go a little out of our way to see if we could procure one of those ducks; so, directing Peterkin to go straight to the shore and kindle a fire, we separated, promising to rejoin him speedily. But we did not find the ducks. We were about to retrace our steps, when we were arrested by one of the strangest sights that we had yet beheld.

Just in front of us grew a superb tree – the largest we had

yet seen on the island. Its trunk was at least five feet in diameter, with a smooth grey bark; above this the spreading branches were clothed with light green leaves, amid which were clusters of bright yellow fruit, so numerous as to weigh down the boughs with their great weight. This fruit seemed to be of the plum species, of an oblong form. The ground at the foot of this tree was thickly strewn with the fallen fruit, in the midst of which lay sleeping at least twenty hogs of all ages and sizes, apparently quite surfeited with a recent banquet.

Jack and I could scarce restrain our laughter as we gazed at these coarse, fat, ill-looking animals, while they lay snoring heavily.

'Now, Ralph,' said Jack, in a low whisper, 'put a stone in your sling – a good big one – and let fly at that fat fellow with his back toward you. I'll try to put an arrow into yon little pig.'

'Don't you think we had better put them up first?' I whispered. 'It seems cruel to kill them while asleep.'

'If I wanted *sport*, Ralph, I would certainly set them up; but as we only want *pork*, we'll let them lie. Besides, we're not sure of killing them; so, fire away.'

Thus admonished, I slung my stone with so good aim that it went bang against the hog's flank as if against the head of a drum; but it had no other effect than that of causing the animal to start to its feet, with a frightful yell of surprise, and scamper away. At the same instant Jack's bow twanged and the arrow pinned the little pig to the ground by the ear.

'I've missed, after all,' cried Jack, darting forward with uplifted axe, while the little pig uttered a loud squeal, tore the arrow from the ground, and ran away with it, along with the whole drove, into the bushes and disappeared, though we heard them screaming long afterwards in the distance.

'That's very provoking, now,' said Jack. 'Well, we must make haste and rejoin Peterkin. It's getting late.' We threaded our way quickly through the woods towards the shore.

When we reached it, we found wood laid out, the fire lighted and beginning to kindle up, but Peterkin was nowhere to be found. We wondered very much at this; but Jack suggested that he might have gone to fetch water; so he gave a shout to let him know that we had arrived, and sat down upon a rock, while I threw off my jacket and seized the axe, intending to split up one or two billets of wood. But I had scarce moved from the spot when, in the distance, we heard a most appalling shriek, which was followed up by a chorus of yells from the hogs, and a loud 'Hurrah!'

'I do believe,' said I, 'that Peterkin has met with the hogs.'

'Hurrah!' shouted Peterkin in the distance.

We soon descried Peterkin walking towards us with a little pig transfixed on the end of his long spear!

'Well done, my boy!' exclaimed Jack, slapping him on the shoulder when he came up. 'You're the best shot amongst us.'

'Look here, Jack!' cried Peterkin, as he disengaged the animal from his spear. 'Do you recognize that hole?' said he, pointing to the pig's ear. 'And are you familiar with this arrow, eh?'

'Well, I declare!' said Jack.

We now set about preparing supper; and a good display we made, when all was laid out on a flat rock in the light of the blazing fire. There was the little pig; then there was the taro-root, the yam, the potato, and six plums; and, lastly, the wood-pigeon. To these Peterkin added a bit of sugar-cane, which he had cut from a little patch of that plant which he had found; 'and,' said he, 'the patch was somewhat in a square form, which convinces me it must have been planted by man.'

'Very likely,' replied Jack. 'From all we have seen, I'm inclined to think that some of the natives must have dwelt here long ago.'

We found no small difficulty in making up our minds how we were to cook the pig. None of us had ever cut one up before, and we did not know exactly how to begin; besides, we had nothing but the axe to do it with, our knife having been forgotten.

At last Jack started up and said: 'Don't let us waste more time talking about it, boys. Hold it up, Peterkin. There, lay the hind leg on this block of wood – so'; and he cut it off, with a large portion of the haunch, at a single blow of the axe. 'Now the other – that's it.' And having cut off the two hind legs, he thrust a sharp-pointed stick through each, and stuck them up before the blaze to roast. The wood-pigeon was then split open, washed clean in salt water, and treated in a similar manner. While these were cooking, we scraped a hole in the sand and ashes under the fire, into which we put our vegetables, and covered them up.

The taro-root was of an oval shape, about ten inches long and four or five thick. It was of a mottled-grey colour, and had a thick rind. We found it somewhat like an Irish potato, and exceedingly good. The yam was roundish, and had a rough brown skin. It was very sweet and well flavoured. The potato was quite sweet and exceedingly palatable, as also were the plums; and, indeed, the pork and pigeon too, when we came to taste them. Altogether this was decidedly the most luxurious supper we had enjoyed for many a day. And so, having eaten our fill, we laid ourselves comfortably down to sleep upon a couch of branches, under the overhanging ledge of a coral rock.

When we awoke on the following morning, we found that the sun was already a good way above the horizon. A heavy supper is not conducive to early rising! Nevertheless, we felt remarkably well, and much disposed to have our breakfast. First we had our customary morning bathe.

We had not advanced on our journey much above a mile or so when, on turning a point that revealed to us a new and beautiful cluster of islands, we were suddenly arrested by the appalling cry which had so alarmed us a few nights before. On hearing the sound, Peterkin instantly threw forward his spear.

'Now, what can it be?' said he, looking round at Jack. 'I tell you, if we are to go on being pulled up in a constant state of horror, the sooner we're out o' this island the better, notwithstanding the yams and lemonade, and pork and plums!'

Peterkin's remark was followed by a repetition of the cry, louder than before.

'It comes from one of these islands,' said Jack.

We all turned our eyes towards the cluster of islands, where, on the largest, we observed curious objects moving on the shore.

'Soldiers they are – that's flat!' cried Peterkin, gazing at them in the utmost amazement.

At the distance from which we saw them, they appeared to be an army of soldiers. There they stood, rank and file, in lines and in squares, marching and countermarching, with blue coats and white trousers. While we were looking at them, the dreadful cry came again over the water, and Peterkin suggested that it must be a regiment sent out to massacre the natives in cold blood. At this remark Jack laughed and said: 'Why, Peterkin, they are penguins!'

'Penguins?' repeated Peterkin.

'Ay, penguins, Peterkin, penguins – nothing more or less than big sea-birds, as you shall see one of these days, when we pay them a visit in our boat, which I mean to set building the moment we return to our bower.'

Now, as we continued on our way, I pondered much over this new discovery, and the singular appearance of these birds, and I began to long to commence our boat, in order that we might go and inspect them more narrowly.

The second night we passed in a manner somewhat similar to the first, at about two-thirds of the way round the island, as we calculated, and we hoped to sleep on the night following at our bower.

Next day we found several more droves of hogs in the woods, but abstained from killing any of them, having more than sufficient for our present necessities. We saw also many of their footprints in this neighbourhood. Among these we also observed the footprints of a smaller animal, which we examined with much care, but could form no certain opinion as to them. Peterkin thought they were those of a little dog, but Jack and I thought differently. We became very curious on this matter, the more so that we observed these footprints to lie scattered about in one locality, as if the animal which had made them was wandering round about in a very irregular manner, and without any object in view. Suddenly we heard a faint cry, and observed a black animal standing in the track before us.

'A wild cat!' cried Jack, fitting an arrow to his bow, and discharging it so hastily that he missed the animal, and hit the earth about half a foot to one side of it. To our surprise the wild cat did not fly, but walked slowly towards the arrow, and snuffed at it.

'That's the most comical wild cat I ever saw!' cried Jack.

'It's a tame wild cat, I think,' said Peterkin.

'I do believe the poor beast is blind,' cried I. 'See, it strikes against the branches as it walks along. It must be a very old one'; and I hastened towards it.

We now found that the poor cat was not only blind, or nearly so, but extremely deaf, as it did not hear our footsteps until we were quite close behind it. Then it sprang round, and, putting up its back and tail, while the black hair stood all on end, uttered a hoarse mew and a fuff.

'Poor thing,' said Peterkin, endeavouring to pat the cat's head. 'Poor pussy; chee, chee, chee; puss, puss, puss; cheetie pussy!'

No sooner did the cat hear these sounds than, advancing eagerly to Peterkin, it allowed itself to be stroked, and rubbed itself against his legs, purring loudly all the time.

'It's no more a wild cat than I am!' cried Peterkin, taking it in his arms. 'It's quite tame. Poor pussy, cheetie pussy!'

We now crowded around Peterkin, and were not a little surprised by the sight of the poor animal's excessive joy. It rubbed its head against Peterkin's cheek, licked his chin, and thrust its head almost violently into his neck, while it purred more loudly than I ever heard a cat purr before. Such demonstrations of joy and affection led us at once to conclude that this poor cat must have known man before, and we conjectured that it had been left either accidentally or by design on the island many years ago. While we were fondling the cat and talking about it, Jack glanced round the open space in the midst of which we stood.

'Hallo!' exclaimed he; 'this looks something like a clearing. The axe has been at work here. Just look at these tree-stumps.'

We now turned to examine these, and found trees that had been cut down here and there, also stumps and broken branches; all of which, however, were completely covered over with moss, and bore evidence of having been in this condition for some years. No human footprints were to be seen, either on the track or among the bushes; but those of the cat were found everywhere. We determined to follow up the track as far as it went, and Peterkin put the cat down; but it seemed to be so weak, and mewed so pitifully, that he took it up again and carried it in his arms, where it fell sound asleep.

About ten yards farther on, the felled trees became more numerous, and the track, diverging to the right, followed for a short space the banks of a stream. Suddenly we came to a spot where once must have been a rude bridge, the stones of which were scattered in the stream. We continued to advance and, a few yards farther on, beheld, under the shelter of some bread-fruit trees, a small hut or cottage. We stood in silent wonder, for there was a deep and most melancholy stillness about the place; and when we did at length speak, it was in subdued whispers. There was a dreariness about this silent, lonely, uninhabited cottage – so strange in its appearance, so old, decayed, and deserted in its aspect – that fell upon our spirits like a thick cloud.

The hut was rude and simple in construction, not more than twelve feet long by ten feet broad, and about seven or eight feet high. It had a small frame in which a window might once have been, but which was now empty. The door was exceedingly low, and formed of rough boards, and the roof was covered with broad coconut and plantain leaves. But every part of it was in a state of the utmost decay. Moss and green matter grew in spots all over it. The woodwork was quite perforated with holes; the roof had nearly fallen in, and appeared to be prevented from doing so altogether by the thick matting of creeping plants and the interlaced branches which years of neglect had allowed to cover it almost entirely.

We lifted the latch and pushed open the door. The latch was made of iron, and almost eaten away with rust. In like condition were also the hinges, which creaked as the door swung back. On entering, we stood and gazed around us, much impressed with the dreary stillness of the room. But what we saw there surprised and shocked us not a little. There was no furniture save a little wooden stool and an iron pot, the latter almost eaten through with rust. In the corner farthest from the door was a low bedstead, on which lay two skeletons, embedded in a little heap of dry dust. With beating hearts we went forward to examine them. One was the skeleton of a man, the other that of a dog, which was extended close beside that of the man, with its head resting on his bosom.

After some time, we began to examine in and around the hut, in order to discover some clue to the name or history of this poor man. But we found nothing – neither a book nor a scrap of paper. We found, however, the decayed remnants of what appeared to have been clothing, and an old axe. But none of these things bore marks of any kind; and, indeed, they were so much decayed as to convince us that they had lain in the condition in which we found them for many years.

This discovery now accounted to us for the tree-stump at the top of the mountain with the initials cut on it; also for the patch of sugar-cane and other traces of man which we had met with. Having no clue whatever to account for the presence of this poor human being in such a lonely spot, we fell to conjecturing what could have brought him there. I was inclined to think that he must have been a shipwrecked

in the sea; well, fill your tank with sea-water, and keep it at that saltness by marking the height at which the water stands on the sides. When it evaporates a little, pour in *fresh* water from the brook till it comes up to the mark, and then it will be right, for the salt does not evaporate with the water. Then, there's lots of seaweed in the sea; well, go and get one or two bits of seaweed, and put them into your tank. Of course the weed must be alive, and growing to little stones; or you can chip a bit off the rocks with the weed sticking to it. Then, if you like, you can throw a little sand and gravel into your tank, and the thing's complete.'

'But hallo! what's this?' said Peterkin. 'I say, Ralph, look here. There's one o' your crabs up to something uncommon. It's performing the most remarkable operation for a crab I ever saw – taking off its coat, I do believe, before going to bed!'

We hastily stooped over the tank, and certainly were not a little amused at the conduct of one of the crabs. We observed its back to split away from the lower part of its body, and out of the gap thus formed came a soft lump which moved and writhed unceasingly. This lump continued to increase in size until it appeared like a bunch of crab's legs: and, indeed, such it proved in very few minutes to be; for the points of the toes were at length extricated from his hole in its back, the legs spread out, the body followed, and the crab walked away quite entire, even to the points of its nipper-claws, leaving a perfectly entire shell behind it.

'Well!' exclaimed Peterkin, drawing a long breath, 'I've *heard* of a man jumping out of his skin and sitting down in his skeleton in order to cool himself, but I never expected to *see* a crab do it!'

We were, in truth, much amazed at this spectacle, and the more so when we observed that the new crab was larger than the crab that it came out of. It was also quite soft, but by next morning its skin had hardened into a good shell.

I considered well the advice which Jack had given me about preparing my tank. So I put his plan in execution, and found it to answer well; for I found that after a little experience had taught me the proper proportion of seaweed and animals to put into a certain amount of water, the tank needed no further attendance; and, moreover, I did not require ever afterwards to renew or change the sea-water, but only to add a very little fresh water from the brook as the other evaporated.

For many days after this, while Peterkin and Jack were busily employed in building a little boat out of the curious natural planks of the chestnut tree, I spent much of my time in examining with the burning-glass the marvellous operations going on in my tank. Here I saw those anemones which cling, like little red, yellow, and green blobs of jelly, to the rocks, put forth, as it were, a multitude of arms and wait till little fish or other small animalcules unwarily touched them, when they would instantly seize them, fold arm after arm around their victims, and so engulf them in their stomachs. Here I saw the ceaseless working of those little coral insects whose efforts have encrusted the islands of the Pacific with vast rocks, and surrounded them with enormous reefs. Here I saw curious little barnacles opening a hole in their backs and constantly putting out a thin feathery hand, with which, I doubt not, they dragged their food into their mouths. Here, also, I saw those crabs which have shells only on the front of their bodies, but no shell whatever on their remarkably tender tails, so that, in order to find a protection to them, they thrust them into the empty shells of wilks, or some such fish, and when they grow too big for one, change into another. All this I saw, and a great deal more, by means of my tank and my burning-glass.

CHAPTER VI

'Come, Jack,' cried Peterkin one morning, 'let's be jolly today, and do something vigorous. I'm quite tired of hammering and bammering, hewing and screwing, cutting and butting, at that little boat of ours; let us go on an excursion to the mountain-top, or have a hunt after the wild ducks, or make a dash at the pigs. I'm flat as a pancake; in fact, I want something to rouse me, to toss me up, as it were. Eh! What do you say to it?'

'Well,' answered Jack, 'if that's what you want, I would recommend you to make an excursion to the water-spouts; the last one we had to do with tossed you up a considerable height; perhaps the next will send you higher!'

'By the by,' said I, interrupting their conversation, 'I am reminded by this that we have not yet discovered the nature of yon curious appearance that we saw near the water-spouts. Perhaps it would be well to go for that purpose.'

'Well, then, let us away to the water-spouts,' cried Jack, going up to the bower for his bow and arrows; 'and bring your spear, Peterkin. It may be useful.'

We sallied forth eagerly in the direction of the water-spout rocks, which were not far off. On arriving there we hastened down to the edge of the rocks, and gazed over into the sea, where we observed the pale-green object still distinctly visible, moving its tail slowly to and fro in the water.

'Most remarkable!' said Jack.

'Exceedingly curious,' said I.

'Beats everything!' said Peterkin. 'Now, Jack,' he added, 'you made such a poor figure in your last attempt to stick that object, that I would advise you to let me try it. If it has got a heart at all, I'll engage to send my spear right through the core of it.'

'Fire away, then, my boy,' replied Jack with a laugh.

Peterkin immediately took the spear, poised it for a second or two above his head, then darted it like an arrow into the sea. Down it went straight into the centre of the green object, passed quite through it, and came up immediately afterwards, pure and unsullied, while the mysterious tail moved quietly as before!

'Now,' said Peterkin, gravely, 'that brute is a heartless monster; I'll have nothing more to do with it.'

'I'm pretty sure now,' said Jack, 'that it is merely a phosphoric light; but I must say I'm puzzled as its staying always in that exact spot.'

I also was much puzzled, and inclined to think with Jack that it must be phosphoric light. 'But,' said I, 'there is nothing to hinder us from diving down to it, now that we are sure it is not a shark.'

'True,' returned Jack, stripping off his clothes; 'I'll go down, Ralph, as I'm better at diving than you are.' Jack stepped forward, joined his hands above his head, and plunged into the sea. For a second or two the spray caused by his dive hid him from view, then the water became still, and we saw him swimming far down in the midst of the green object. Suddenly he sank below it, and vanished altogether from our sight! We gazed anxiously down at the spot where he had disappeared, expecting every moment to see him rise again for breath; but fully a minute passed, and still he did not reappear. Two minutes passed! And then a flood of alarm rushed in upon my soul, when I considered that Jack had never stayed under water more than a minute at a time; indeed seldom so long.

'Oh, Peterkin!' I said, in a voice that trembled with increasing anxiety. 'Something has happened. It is more than three minutes now!' But Peterkin did not answer, and I observed that he was gazing down into the water with a look of intense anxiety, his face overspread with deadly paleness.

Suddenly he sprang to his feet and rushed about in a frantic state, wringing his hands, and exclaiming: 'Oh, Jack, Jack! It must have been a shark, and he is gone for ever!'

For the next five minutes the intensity of my feelings almost bereft me of my senses. But I was recalled to myself by Peterkin seizing me by the shoulder while he exclaimed: 'Ralph! Ralph! Perhaps he has only fainted. Dive for him, Ralph!'

It seemed strange that this did not occur to me sooner. In a moment I rushed to the edge of the rocks, and, without waiting to throw off my garments, was on the point to spring into the waves, when I observed something black rising up through the green object. In another moment Jack's head rose to the surface, and he gave a wild shout. Now we were almost as much amazed at seeing him reappear, well and strong, as we had been at first at his non-appearance; for, to the best of our judgement, he had been nearly ten minutes under water, perhaps longer. It was therefore with a feeling akin to awe that I assisted him to clamber up the steep rocks. But no such feeling affected Peterkin. No sooner did Jack gain the rocks and seat himself on one, panting for breath, than he threw his arms round his neck. 'Oh, Jack, Jack!' said he, 'where were you? What kept you so long?'

After a few moments Peterkin became composed enough to sit still and listen to Jack's explanation.

'Now, lads,' said Jack, 'yon green object is not a shark; it is a stream of light issuing from a cave in the rocks. Just after I made my dive, I observed that this light came from the side of the rock above which we are now sitting; so I struck out for it, and saw an opening into some place that appeared to be luminous within. For one instant I paused to think whether I ought to venture. Then I dashed into it. It happened in the space of a few seconds, so that I knew I had wind enough to bring me out o' the hole and up to the surface again. Well, I was just on the point of turning – for I began to feel a little uncomfortable in such a place – when it seemed to me as if there was a faint light right above me. I darted upwards, and found my head out of water. This relieved me greatly, for I now felt that I could take in air enough to return the way I came. Then it all at once occurred to me that I might not be able to find the way out again; but, on glancing downwards, my mind was put quite at rest by seeing the green light below me streaming into the cave, just like the light that we had seen streaming out of it, only what I now saw was much brighter.

'At first I could scarcely see anything as I gazed around me, it was so dark; but gradually my eyes became accustomed to it, and I found I was in a huge cave. The ceiling just above me was also visible, and I fancied that I could perceive beautiful glittering objects there, but the farther end of the cave was shrouded in darkness. While I was looking around me in great wonder, it came into my head that you two would think I was drowned; so I plunged down through the passage again in a great hurry, rose to the surface, and – here I am!'

When Jack concluded his recital of what he had seen in this remarkable cave, I could not rest satisfied till I had dived down to see it; which I did, but found it so dark, as Jack had said, that I could scarcely see anything. When I returned, we had a long conversation about it, during which I observed that Peterkin had a most lugubrious expression.

'What's the matter, Peterkin?' said I.

'The matter?' he replied. 'It's all very well for you two to be talking away like mermaids about the wonders of this cave, but you know I must be content to hear about it, while you are enjoying yourselves down there. It's really too bad.'

'I'm very sorry for you, Peterkin,' said Jack, 'but we cannot help you. If you would only learn to dive –'

'Learn to fly, you might as well say!' retorted Peterkin.

'If you would only consent to keep still,' said I, 'we would take you down with us in ten seconds.'

'Hum!' returned Peterkin; 'suppose a salamander was to propose to you "only to keep still," and he would carry you through a blazing fire in a few seconds, what would you say?'

We both laughed and shook our heads, for it was evident

that nothing was to be made of Peterkin in the water. But we could not rest satisfied till we had seen more of this cave; so Jack and I determined to try if we could take down a torch with us, and set fire to it in the cavern. This we found to be an undertaking of no small difficulty; but we accomplished it at last by the following means: first, we made a torch of a very inflammable nature out of the bark of a certain tree, which we cut into strips, and, after twisting, cemented together with a kind of resin or gum, which we obtained from another tree. This we wrapped up in a great number of plies of coconut cloth, so that we were confident it could not get wet. Then we took a small piece of the tinder, which we had carefully treasured up lest we should require it when the sun should fail us; also, we rolled up some dry grass and a few chips, which, with a little bow and drill we made into another bundle, and wrapped it up in coconut cloth. When all was ready we laid aside our garments, with the exception of our trousers, which, as we did not know what rough scraping against the rocks we might be subjected to, we kept on.

Then we advanced to the edge of the rocks, Jack carrying one bundle, with the torch; I the other, with the things for producing fire.

'Now don't worry, Peterkin, should we be gone some time,' said Jack; 'we'll be sure to return in half an hour at the very latest, however interesting the cave should be, that we may relieve your mind.'

'Farewell!' said Peterkin, coming up to us with a look of deep but pretended solemnity, while he shook hands. 'Farewell! and while you are gone I shall repose my weary limbs under the shelter of this bush.' So saying, Peterkin turned from us, and cast himself upon the ground with a look of melancholy resignation, accompanied by a wink. Jack and I laughed, and, springing from the rocks together, plunged head first into the sea.

We gained the interior of the submarine cave without difficulty, and, emerging from the waves, supported ourselves for some time by treading water, while we held the two bundles above our heads. This we did in order to let our eyes become accustomed to the obscurity. Then we swam to a shelving rock, and landed in safety. Having wrung the water from our trousers, and dried ourselves as well as we could, we ignited the torch without difficulty in a few minutes; and no sooner did it flare up than we were struck dumb with the wonderful objects revealed to our gaze. The roof of the cavern just above us seemed to be about ten feet high, but grew higher as it receded into the distance, until it was lost in darkness. It seemed to be made of coral, and was supported by massive columns of the same material. Immense icicles hung from it in various places. These, however, were formed, not of ice, but of a species of limestone, which seemed to flow in a liquid form towards the point of each, where it became solid. A good many drops fell, however, to the rock below, and these formed little cones, which rose to meet the points above. Some of them had already met, and thus we saw how the pillars were formed, which at first seemed as if they had been placed there by some human architect to support the roof.

As we advanced farther in, we saw that the floor was composed of the same material as the pillars; and it presented the curious appearance of ripples, such as are formed on water when gently ruffled by the wind. There were several openings on either hand in the walls, which seemed to lead into other caverns; but these we did not explore at this time. We also observed that the ceiling was curiously marked in many places, as if it were the fretwork of a noble cathedral; and the walls, as well as the roof, sparkled in the light of our torch, and threw back gleams and flashes, as if they were covered with precious stones. Although we proceeded far into this cavern, we did not come to the end of it; and we were obliged to return more speedily than we would otherwise have done, as our torch was nearly expended. We did not see any openings in the roof, or any indications of places whereby light might enter; but near the entrance to the cavern stood an immense mass of pure white coral rock, which caught and threw back the little light that found an entrance through the cave's mouth, and thus produced, we conjectured, the pale-green object which had first attracted our attention. We concluded, also, that the reflecting power of this rock was that which gave forth the dim light that faintly illumined the first part of the cave.

Before diving through the passage again we extinguished the small piece of our torch that remained, and left it in a dry spot.

'Now, Ralph, are you ready?' said Jack, in a low voice that seemed to echo up into the dome above.

'Quite ready.'

'Come along, then,' said he; and, plunging off the ledge of the rock into the water, we dived through the narrow entrance. In a few seconds we were panting on the rocks above.

It was quite a relief to us to breathe the pure air and enjoy the sunshine after our long ramble in the Diamond Cave, as we named it; for, although we did not stay more than half an hour away, it seemed to us much longer. During our walk home, we did our best to satisfy the curiosity of poor Peterkin, who regretted bitterly his inability to dive.

We condoled with him as we best could. Had there been any great rise or fall in the tide of these seas, we might perhaps have found it possible to take him down with us at low water; but as the tide never rose or fell more than eighteen inches or two feet, this was impossible.

This peculiarity of the tide – its slight rise and fall – had not attracted our observation till some time after our residence on the island. Neither had we observed another curious circumstance until we had been some time there. This was the fact that the tide rose and fell with constant regularity, instead of being affected by the changes of the moon as in our own country. Every day and every night, at twelve o'clock precisely, the tide is at the full; and at six o'clock every morning and evening it is ebb. Of course we had to guess the hour of twelve midnight, and I think we could do this pretty correctly; but in regard to twelve noon we were quite positive, because we easily found the highest point that the sun reached in the sky, by placing ourselves at a certain spot whence we observed the sharp summit of a cliff resting against the sky, just where the sun passed.

Jack and I were surprised that we had not noticed this the first few days of our residence here, and could only account for it by our being so much taken up with the more obvious wonders of our novel situation.

We had much serious conversation on the tides; and Jack told us, in his own quiet way, that these tides did great good to the world in many ways, particularly in the way of cleansing the shores of the land, and carrying off the filth that was constantly poured into the sea therefrom; which, Peterkin suggested, was remarkably *tidy* of it to do. Poor Peterkin could never let slip an opportunity to joke, however inopportune it might be: which at first we found rather a disagreeable propensity, as it often interrupted the flow of very agreeable conversation; but we became so used to it at last that we found it no interruption whatever. I must not misrepresent Peterkin. We often found, to our surprise, that he knew many things which we did not; and I also observed that those things which he learned from experience were never forgotten.

I may here remark on another curious natural phenomenon. We found that there was little or no twilight in this island. When we first landed, we used to sit down on some rocky point at the close of our day's work, to enjoy the evening breeze; but no sooner had the sun sunk below the horizon than all became suddenly dark. This rendered it necessary that we should watch the sun when we happened to be out hunting, for to be suddenly left in the dark while in the woods was very perplexing, as, although the stars shone with great beauty and brilliancy, they could not pierce through the thick umbrageous boughs above our heads.

But, to return: after having told all we could to Peterkin about the Diamond Cave under Spouting Cliff, as we named the locality, we were wending our way rapidly homewards, when a grunt and a squeal were borne down by the land breeze to our ears.

Peterkin started convulsively, and levelled his spear.

'Hist!' cried Jack; 'these are your friends, Peterkin. They must have come over expressly to pay you a friendly visit, for it is the first time we have seen them on this side of the island.'

'Come along!' cried Peterkin, hurrying towards the wood.

Another grunt and half a dozen squeals, much louder than before, came down the valley. At this time we were just opposite the small vale which lay between the Valley of the Wreck and Spouting Cliff.

'I say, Peterkin,' cried Jack, in a hoarse whisper.

'Well, what is't?'

'Stay a bit, man. These grunters are just up there on the hillside. If you go and stand with Ralph in the lee of yon cliff, I'll cut round behind and drive them through the gorge, so that you'll have a better chance of picking out a good one. Now, mind you pitch into a fat young pig, Peterkin,' added Jack, as he sprang into the bushes.

'Won't I, just!' said Peterkin, licking his lips, as we took our station beside the cliff. 'I feel quite a tender affection for young pigs.'

'There they come!' cried I, as a terrific yell from Jack sent the whole herd screaming down the hill. Peterkin crept a short way up a very steep grassy mound, in order to get a better view of the hogs before they came up; and just as he raised his head above its summit, two little pigs rushed over the top with the utmost precipitation. One of these brushed close past Peterkin's ear; the other, unable to arrest its head-long flight, went, as Peterkin himself afterwards expressed it, 'bash' into his arms with a sudden squeal, and both of them rolled violently down to the foot of the mound. No sooner was this reached than the little pig recovered its feet, tossed up its tail, and fled shrieking from the spot. But I slung a large stone after it, which hit it behind the ear, and felled it to the earth.

'Capital, Ralph!' cried Peterkin, who, to my surprise and relief had risen to his feet. Apparently unhurt, though much dishevelled, he rushed franticly towards the gorge, which the yells of the hogs told us they were now approaching. I had made up my mind that I would abstain from killing another, as, if Peterkin should be successful, two were more than sufficient for our wants at the present time. Suddenly they all burst forth – two or three little round ones in advance, and an enormous old sow with a drove of hogs at her heels.

'Now, Peterkin,' said I, 'there's a nice little fat one; just spear it.'

But Peterkin did not move; he allowed it to pass unharmed. I looked at him in surprise, and saw that his lips were compressed and his eyebrows knitted, as if he were about to fight with some awful enemy.

'What is it?' I enquired, with some trepidation.

Suddenly he levelled his spear, darted forward, and, with a yell that nearly froze the blood in my veins, stabbed the old sow to the heart. Nay, so vigorously was it done that the spear went in at one side and came out at the other!

'Oh, Peterkin!' said I, going up to him. 'What have you done?'

'Done? I've killed their great-great-grandmother, that's all,' said he, looking with a somewhat awestruck expression at the transfixed animal.

'Hallo! what's this?' said Jack, as he came up. 'Why, Peterkin, you must be fond of a tough chop. If you mean to eat this old hog, she'll try your jaws, I warrant. What possessed you to stick *her*, Peterkin?'

'Why, the fact is I want a pair of shoes.'

'What have your shoes to do with the old hog?' said I, smiling.

'My present shoes have certainly nothing to do with her,' replied Peterkin; 'nevertheless she will have a good deal to do with my future shoes. The fact is, when I saw you floor that pig so neatly, Ralph, it struck me that there was little use in killing another. Then I remembered all at once that I had long wanted some leather or tough substance to make shoes of, and this old grandmother seemed so tough that I just made up my mind to stick her, and you see I've done it!'

'That you certainly have, Peterkin,' said Jack, as he was examining the transfixed animal.

We now considered how we were to carry our game home, for, although the distance was short, the hog was very heavy. At length we hit on the plan of tying its four feet together, and passing the spear handle between them. Jack took one end on his shoulder, I took the other on mine, and Peterkin carried the small pig.

Thus we returned in triumph to our bower, laden, as Peterkin remarked, with the spoils of a noble hunt. He afterwards spoke in similarly glowing terms in reference to the supper that followed.

CHAPTER VII

For many days after this Jack applied himself to the construction of our boat, which at length began to look somewhat like one. But only those who have had the thing to do can entertain a right idea of the difficulty involved in such an undertaking, with no other implements than an axe, a bit of hoop iron, a sail-needle, and a broken penknife. But Jack did it. He was of that disposition which *will* not be conquered.

As this boat was a curiosity in its way, a few words here relative to the manner of its construction may not be amiss.

I have already mentioned the chestnut tree with its wonderful buttresses or planks. This tree, then, furnished us with the chief part of our material. First of all Jack sought out a limb of a tree of such a form and size as, while it should form the keel, a bend at either end should form the stem and stern posts. Such a piece, however, was not easy to obtain, but at last he procured it, by rooting up a small tree which had a branch growing at the proper angle about ten feet up its stem, with two strong roots growing in such a form as enabled him to make a flat-sterned boat. This placed, he procured three branching roots of suitable size, which he fitted to the keel at equal distances, thus forming three strong ribs. Now, the squaring and shaping of these, and the cutting of the grooves in the keel, was an easy enough matter, as it was all work for the axe, in the use of which Jack was becoming wonderfully expert; but it was quite a different affair when he came to nailing the ribs to the keel, for we had no instrument capable of boring a large hole, and no nails to fasten them with. We were, indeed, much perplexed here; but Jack at length devised an instrument that served very well. He took the remainder of our hoop iron and beat it into the form of a pipe or cylinder, about as thick as a man's finger. This he did by means of our axe and the old rusty axe we had found at the house of the poor man at the other side of the island. This, when made red hot, bored slowly through the timbers; and, the better to retain the heat, Jack shut up one end of it and filled it with sand. True, the work was very slowly done, but it mattered not – we had little else to do. Two holes were bored in each timber, about an inch and a half apart, and also down into the keel, but not quite through. Into these were placed stout pegs made of a tree called iron-wood; and, when they were hammered well home, the timbers were as firmly fixed as if they had been nailed with iron.

The gunwales, which were very stout, were fixed in a similar manner. But, besides the wooden nails, they were firmly lashed to the stem and stern posts and ribs by means of a species of cordage which we had contrived to make out of the fibrous husk of the coconut. This husk was very tough, and when a number of the threads were joined together they formed excellent cordage. At first we tied the different lengths together, but this was such a clumsy and awkward complication of knots, that we contrived, by careful inter-lacing of the ends together before twisting, to make good cordage of any size or length we chose. Of course it cost us much time and infinite labour, but Jack kept up our spirits when we grew weary, and so all that we required was at last constructed.

Planks were now cut off the chestnut trees of about an inch thick. These were dressed with the axe – but clumsily, for an axe is ill adapted for such work. Five of these planks on each side were sufficient, and we formed the boat in a very rounded, barrel-like shape, in order to have as little twisting of the planks as possible; for, although we could easily bend them, we could not easily twist them. Having no nails to rivet the planks with, we threw aside the ordinary fashion of boat-building and adopted one of our own. The planks were therefore placed on each other's edges, and sewed together with the tough cordage already mentioned. They were also thus sewed to the stem, the stern, and the keel. Each stitch or tie was six inches apart, and was formed thus: three holes were bored in the upper plank and three in the lower – the holes being above each other, that is, in a vertical line. Through these holes the cord was passed, and, when tied, formed a powerful stitch of three-ply. Besides this, we placed between the edges of the planks, layers of coconut fibre, which, as it swelled when wetted, would, we hoped, make our little vessel watertight. But we also collected a large quantity of pitch from the bread-fruit tree, with which, when boiled in our old iron pot, we painted the whole of the inside of the boat, and, while it was yet hot, placed large pieces of coconut cloth on it, and then gave it another coat above that. Thus the interior was covered with a tough watertight material; while the exterior, being uncovered, and so exposed to the swelling action of the water, was, we hoped, likely to keep the boat quite dry. I may add that our hopes were not disappointed.

While Jack was thus engaged, Peterkin and I sometimes assisted him, but we more frequently went ahunting on the extensive mud-flats at the entrance of the long valley nearest to our bower. Here we found large flocks of ducks of various kinds. On these occasions we took the bow and the sling, with both of which we were often successful, though I must confess I was the least so. Our suppers were thus pleasantly varied.

I must also add that the poor old cat which we had brought home had always a liberal share of our good things, and so well was it looked after, especially by Peterkin, that it recovered much of its former strength, and seemed to improve in sight as well as hearing.

The large flat stone, or rock of coral, which stood just in front of the entrance to our bower, was our table. Sometimes we sat down at this table to a feast consisting of hot rolls – as Peterkin called the newly baked bread-fruit – a roast pig, roast duck, boiled and roasted yams, coconuts, taro, and sweet potatoes; which we followed up with a dessert of plums, apples, and plantains – the last being a large-sized and delightful fruit. These luxurious feasts were usually washed down with coconut lemonade.

One day Jack came up from the beach, and, flinging down his axe, exclaimed: 'There, lads, the boat's finished at last! So we've nothing to do now but shape two pairs of oars, and then we may put to sea as soon as we like.'

This piece of news threw us into a state of great joy; for the boat had taken so long that we did not expect it to be ready for at least two or three weeks. But Jack had wrought hard and said nothing, in order to surprise us.

'My dear fellow,' cried Peterkin, 'you're a perfect trump. But why did you not tell us it was so nearly ready? Won't we have a jolly sail tomorrow, eh?'

'Don't talk so much, Peterkin,' said Jack; 'and, pray, hand me a bit of that pig.'

'Certainly,' cried Peterkin, seizing the axe; 'what part will you have – a leg, or a shoulder, or a piece of the breast; which?'

'A hind leg, if you please,' answered Jack; 'and, pray, be so good as to include the tail.'

'With all my heart,' said Peterkin, exchanging the axe for his hoop-iron knife, with which he cut off the desired portion.

'Well,' continued Peterkin, 'I was talking of a sail to-morrow. Can't we have one, Jack?'

'No,' replied Jack, 'we can't have a sail, but I hope we shall have a row, as I intend to work hard at the oars this after-noon, and, if we can't get them finished by sunset we'll light our candle-nuts, and turn them out before we turn into bed.'

'Very good,' said Peterkin, tossing a lump of pork to the cat, who received it with a mew of satisfaction. 'I'll help you, if I can.'

'Afterwards,' continued Jack, 'we will make a sail out of the coconut cloth, and rig up a mast, and then we shall be able to sail to some of the other islands, and visit our old friends the penguins.'

After dinner we set about making the oars in good earnest. Jack went into the woods and blocked them roughly out with the axe, and I smoothed them down with the knife, while Peterkin remained in the bower, spinning, or, rather, twisting some strong thick cordage with which to fasten them to the boat.

We worked hard and rapidly, so that, when the sun went down, Jack and I returned to the bower with four stout oars, which required little to be done to them save a slight polishing with the knife.

After supper we retired to rest and to dream of wonderful adventures in our little boat, and distant voyages upon the sea.

It was a bright, clear, beautiful morning when we first launched our little boat and rowed out upon the placid waters of the lagoon. Not a breath of wind ruffled the surface of the deep. Not a cloud spotted the deep blue sky. The sun was just rising from the Pacific and tipping the mountain-tops with a red glow. The sea was shining like a sheet of glass, and the bright seaweeds and the brilliant corals shone in the depths of that pellucid water, as we rowed over it, like rare and precious gems.

At first, in the strength of our delight, we rowed hither and thither without aim or object. But after that we began to consider what we should do.

'I vote that we row to the reef,' cried Peterkin.

'And I vote that we visit the islands within the lagoon,' said I.

'And I vote we do both,' cried Jack, 'so pull away, boys.'

We had made four oars, but our boat was so small that only two were necessary. The extra pair were reserved in case any accident should happen to the others. It was therefore only needful that two of us should row, while the third steered, by means of an oar, and relieved the rowers occasionally.

First we landed on one of the small islands and ran all over it, but saw nothing worthy of particular notice. Then we landed on a larger island, on which were growing a few coconut trees. Not having eaten anything that morning, we gathered a few of the nuts and breakfasted. After this we pulled straight out to sea and landed on the coral reef.

This was indeed a novel and interesting sight to us. We had now been so long on shore that we had almost forgotten the appearance of breakers, for there were none within the lagoon; but now, as we stood beside the foam-crested billow of the open sea, all the enthusiasm of the sailor was awakened in our breasts.

This huge, ceaseless breaker that burst in thunder at our feet was a much larger and more sublime object than we had imagined it to be. It rose many yards above the level of the sea, and could be seen approaching at some distance from the reef. Slowly and majestically it came on, acquiring greater volume and velocity as it advanced, until it assumed the form of a clear watery arch, which sparkled in the bright sun. On it came with solemn majesty – the upper edge lipped gently over, and it fell with a roar that seemed as though the heart of Ocean were broken in the crash of tumultuous water.

We gazed long and wonderingly at this great sight. This wave broke in many places over the reef and scattered some of its spray into the lagoon, but in most places the reef was sufficiently broad and elevated to check its entire force. In many places the coral rocks were covered with vegetation – the beginning of future islands. Thus, on this reef, we came to perceive how most of the small islands of those seas are formed. On one part we saw the spray of the breaker washing over the rocks, and millions of little, active, busy creatures continuing the work of building up this living rampart. At another place, which was just a little too high for the waves to wash over it, the coral insects were all dead; for we found that they never did their work above water. Again, in other spots the ceaseless lashing of the sea had broken the dead coral in pieces, and cast it up in the form of sand. Here sea-birds had alighted, little pieces of seaweed and stray bits of wood had been washed up, seeds of plants had been carried by the wind, and a few lovely blades of bright green had already sprung up, which, when they died, would increase the size and fertility of these emeralds of Ocean. At other places these islets had grown apace, and were shaded by one or two coconut trees, which grew, literally, in the sand, and were constantly washed by the ocean spray.

Having satisfied our curiosity and enjoyed ourselves during the whole day, in our little boat, we returned, somewhat wearied, and rather hungry, to our bower.

'Now,' said Jack, 'as our boat answers so well, we will get a mast and sail made immediately.'

'So we will,' cried Peterkin, as we all assisted to drag the boat above high-water mark; 'we'll light our candle and set about it this very night. Hurrah, my boys, pull away!'

As we dragged our boat, we observed that she grated heavily on her keel; and, as the sands were in this place mingled with broken coral rocks, we saw portions of the wood being scraped off.

'Hallo!' cried Jack, on seeing this. 'That won't do. Our keel will be worn off in no time at this rate.'

'So it will,' said I, pondering deeply as to how this might be prevented. 'It seems to me, Jack,' I added, 'that it is impossible to prevent the keel being worn off thus.'

'Impossible!' cried Peterkin. 'My dear Ralph, you are mistaken; there is nothing so easy.'

'How?' I enquired, in some surprise.

'Why, by not using the boat at all!' replied Peterkin.

'Hold your impudent tongue, Peterkin,' said Jack, as he shouldered the oars; 'come along with me and I'll give you work to do. In the first place, you will go and collect coconut fibre, and set to work to make sewing twine with it –'

'Please, captain,' interrupted Peterkin, 'I've got lots of it made already.'

'Very well,' continued Jack; 'then you'll help Ralph to

collect coconut cloth, and cut it into shape, after which we'll make a sail of it. I'll see to getting the mast and the gearing; so let's to work.'

And to work we went right busily, so that in three days from that time we had set up a mast and sail, with the necessary rigging, in our little boat. The sail was not, indeed, very handsome to look at, as it was formed of a number of oblong patches of cloth; but we had sewed it well by means of our sail-needle, so that it was strong, which was the chief point. Jack had also overcome the difficulty about the keel, by pinning to it a *false* keel. This was a piece of tough wood, of the same length and width as the real keel, and about five inches deep. He made it of this depth because the boat would be thereby rendered not only much more safe, but more able to beat against the wind; which, in a sea where the trade winds blow so long and so steadily in one direction, was a matter of great importance. This piece of wood was pegged very firmly to the keel.

The mast and sail answered excellently; and we now sailed about in the lagoon with great delight, and examined with much interest the appearance of our island from a distance. We gazed into the depths of the water, and watched for hours the gambols of the curious and bright-coloured fish among the corals and seaweed. Peterkin also made a fishing line, and Jack constructed a number of hooks, some of which were very good, others remarkably bad. Some of these hooks were made of iron-wood, which did pretty well, the wood being extremely hard, and Jack made them very thick and large. Fish there are not particular. Some of the crooked bones in fish-heads also answered for this purpose pretty well. But that which formed our best and most serviceable hook was the brass finger-ring belonging to Jack. It gave him not a little trouble to manufacture it. First he cut it with the axe; then twisted it into the form of a hook. The barb took him several hours to cut. He did it by means of constant sawing with the broken penknife. As for the point, an hour's rubbing on a piece of sandstone made an excellent one.

Multitudes of fish were day after day drawn into our boat by means of the brass hook. Peterkin always caught them – he derived much pleasure from fishing – while Jack and I found ample amusement in looking on, also in gazing down at the coral groves, and in baiting the hook. Among the fish that we saw, but did not catch, were porpoises and sword-fish, whales and sharks. The porpoises came frequently into our lagoons in shoals, and amused us by their bold leaps into the air, and their playful gambols in the sea. The sword-fish were wonderful creatures, some of them apparently ten feet in length, with an ivory spear, six or eight feet long, project-ing from their noses. We often saw them darting after other fish, and no doubt they sometimes killed them with their ivory swords.

Sharks did not often appear; but we took care never again to bathe in deep water without leaving one of our number in the boat to give us warning. As for the whales, they never came into our lagoon, but we frequently saw them spouting in the deep water beyond the reef. I shall never forget my surprise the first day I saw one of these huge monsters close to me. We had been rambling about on the reef during the morning, and were about to re-embark in our little boat, to return home, when a loud blowing sound caused us to wheel rapidly round. We were just in time to see a shower of spray falling, and the flukes or tail of some monstrous fish dis-appear in the sea a few hundred yards off. We waited some time to see if he would rise again. As we stood, the sea seemed to open up at our very feet; an immense spout of water was sent with a snort high into the air, and the huge blunt head of a sperm whale arose before us. It was so large that it could easily have taken our little boat, along with ourselves, into its mouth! It plunged slowly back into the sea, like a large ship foundering, and struck the water with its tail so forcibly as to cause a sound like a cannon shot.

During these delightful fishing and boating excursions we caught a good many eels, which we found very good to eat. We also found turtles among the coral rocks, and made excellent soup in our iron kettle. Moreover, we discovered many shrimps and prawns, so that we had no lack of variety in our food.

CHAPTER VIII

One day we were sitting on the rocks at Spouting Cliff, and talking of an excursion which we intended to make to Penguin Island the next day.

'I think,' said Jack, 'that you had better remain at home, Peterkin, to take care of the cat; for I'm sure the hogs will be at it in your absence, out of revenge for your killing their great-grandmother so recklessly.'

'Stay at home?' cried Peterkin. 'My dear fellow, you would certainly lose your way, or get upset, if I were not there to take care of you.'

'Ah, true,' said Jack, gravely, 'that did not occur to me; no doubt you must go. Our boat does require a good deal of ballast; and all that you say, Peterkin, carries so much weight with it, that we won't need stones if you go.'

Now, while my companions were talking, a notable event occurred. While we were talking we noticed a dark line, like a low cloud or fog-bank, on the seaward horizon. The day was a fine one, though cloudy, and a gentle breeze was blowing, but the sea was not rougher, or the breaker on the reef higher, than usual. At first we thought that this looked like a thunder-cloud; and we supposed that a storm must be approaching. Gradually, however, this line seemed to draw nearer, without spreading up over the sky, as would certainly have been the case if it had been a storm-cloud. Still nearer it came, and soon we saw that it was moving swiftly towards the island; but there was no sound till it reached the islands out at sea. As it passed these islands, we observed, with no little anxiety, that a cloud of white foam encircled them, and burst in spray into the air: it was accompanied by a loud roar. This led us to conjecture that the approaching object was an enormous wave. When it approached the outer reef we were awestruck with its unusual magnitude; and we sprang to our feet, and clambered hastily up to the highest point of the precipice, under an indefinable feeling of fear.

The reef opposite Spouting Cliff was very near to the shore, while, just in front of the bower, it was at a considerable distance out to sea. Owing to this formation, the wave reached the reef at the latter point before it struck at the foot of Spouting Cliff. The instant it touched the reef we became aware of its awful magnitude. It burst completely over the reef at all points, with a roar that seemed louder to me than thunder; and this roar continued for some seconds, while the wave rolled gradually along towards the cliff on which we stood. As its crest reared before us, we felt that we were in great danger, and turned to flee; but we were too late. With a crash that seemed to shake the solid rocks the gigantic billow fell, and instantly the spouting-holes sent up a gush of water-spouts with such force that they shrieked on issuing from their narrow vents. We were stunned and confused by the shock, and so drenched and blinded with spray, that we knew not for a few moments whither to flee for shelter. At length we all three gained an eminence beyond the reach of the water; but what a scene of devastation met our gaze as we looked along the shore! This enormous wave not only burst over the reef, but continued its way across the lagoon, and fell on the sandy beach of the island with such force it passed completely over it and dashed into the woods, levelling the smaller trees and bushes in its headlong course!

On seeing this, Jack said he feared our bower must have been swept away, and that the boat, which was on the beach, must have been utterly destroyed. Our hearts sank as we thought of this, and we hastened round through the woods towards our home. On reaching it we found, to our great relief, that the force of the wave had been expended just before reaching the bower; but the entrance to it was almost blocked up by the torn-up bushes and tangled heaps of seaweed. Having satisfied ourselves as to the bower, we hurried to the spot where the boat had been left; but no boat was there!

'It may have been washed up into the woods,' said Jack, hurrying up the beach as he spoke. Still, no boat was to be seen, and we were about to give ourselves over to despair, when Peterkin called to Jack and said: 'Jack, my friend, you were once so exceedingly sagacious and wise as to make me acquainted with the fact that coconuts grow upon trees; will you now be so good as to inform me what sort of fruit that is growing on the top of yonder bush?'

We looked towards the bush indicated, and there beheld our little boat snugly nestled among the leaves! We found that the wave had actually borne the boat on its crest from the beach into the woods, and there launched it into the heart of this bush; which was extremely fortunate, for had it been tossed against a rock or a tree, it would have been dashed to pieces, whereas it had not received the smallest injury. It was no easy matter, however, to get it out of the bush and down to the sea again. This cost us two days of hard labour to accomplish.

We had also much ado to clear away the rubbish from before the bower, and spent nearly a week in constant labour before we got the neighbourhood to look as clean and orderly as before.

After we had got our home put to rights and cleared of the debris we again turned our thoughts to paying the penguins a visit. The boat was therefore overhauled and a few repairs done. Then we prepared a supply of provisions, for we intended to be absent at least a night or two, perhaps longer. This took us some time to do, for while Jack was busy with the boat, Peterkin was sent into the woods to spear a hog or two, and had to search long, sometimes, before he found them. Peterkin was usually sent on this errand, when we wanted a pork chop (which was not seldom), because he was so active, and could run so wonderfully fast that he found no difficulty in overtaking the hogs; but, being dreadfully reckless, he almost invariably tumbled over the stumps and stones in the course of his wild chase, and seldom returned home without having knocked the skin off his shins. Once, indeed, a more serious accident happened to him. He had been out all morning alone and did not return at the usual time to dinner. We wondered at this, for Peterkin was always very punctual at the dinner hour. As supper-time drew near we began to be anxious about him, and at length sallied forth to search the woods. For a long time we sought in vain, but a little before dark we came upon the tracks of the hogs, which we followed up until we came to the brow of a rather steep bank or precipice. Looking over this we beheld Peterkin lying in a state of insensibility at the foot, with his cheek resting on the snout of a little pig, which was pinned to the earth by the spear! We were dreadfully alarmed, but hastened to bathe his forehead with water, and had soon the satisfaction of seeing him revive. After we had carried him home he related to us how the thing had happened.

'I walked about all the forenoon,' said he, 'till I was as tired as an old donkey, without seeing a single grunter, not so much as a track of one; but, as I was determined not to return empty-handed, I resolved to go without my dinner, and –'

'What!' exclaimed Jack. 'Did you *really* resolve to do that?'

'Now, Jack, hold your tongue,' returned Peterkin. 'I resolved to push to the head of the small valley, where I felt pretty sure of discovering the hogs. I had scarcely walked half a mile in the direction of the small plum tree we found there the other day, when a squeak fell on my ear. "Ho, ho," said I, "there you go, my boys"; and I hurried up the glen. I soon started them, and singling out a fat pig, ran tilt at him. In a few seconds I was up with him, and stuck my spear right through his dumpy body. Just as I did so, I saw that we were on the edge of a precipice, whether high or low I knew not, but I had been running at such a pace that I could not stop, so the pig and I gave a howl in concert and went plunging over together. I remembered nothing more after that, till I came to my senses and found you bathing my temples, and Ralph wringing his hands over me.'

But although Peterkin was often unfortunate, in the way of getting tumbles, he was successful on the present occasion in hunting, and returned before evening with three very nice little hogs. I, also, was successful in my visit to the mud-flats, where I killed several ducks. So that, when we launched and loaded our boat at sunrise the following morning, we found our store of provisions to be more than sufficient. Part had been cooked the night before, and, on taking note of the different items, we found the account to stand thus:

    10 Bread-fruits (two baked, eight unbaked)
    20 Yams (six roasted, the rest raw)
     6 Taro roots
    50 Fine large plums
     6 Coconuts, ripe
     6 Ditto green (for drinking)
     4 Large ducks and two small ones, raw
     3 Cold roast pigs, with stuffing

We calculated that this supply would last us for several days, but we afterwards found that it was much more than we required, especially in regard to the coconuts, of which we found large supplies wherever we went. However, as Peterkin remarked, it was better to have too much than too little.

It was a very calm sunny morning when we launched forth and rowed over the lagoon towards the outlet in the reef, and passed between the two green islets that guard the entrance. We experienced some difficulty in passing the surf of the breaker, and shipped a good deal of water in the attempt; but, once past the billow, we found ourselves floating placidly on the long oily swell that rose and fell slowly as it rolled over the wide ocean.

Penguin Island lay on the other side of our own island, about a mile beyond the outer reef, and we calculated that it must be at least twenty miles distant by the way we should have to go. We might, indeed, have shortened the way by coasting round our island inside the lagoon, and going out at the passage in the reef nearly opposite to Penguin Island, but we preferred to go by the open sea.

'I wish we had a breeze,' said Jack.

'So do I,' cried Peterkin, resting on his oar and wiping his heated brow; 'pulling is hard work. Oh dear, if we could only catch a hundred or two of these gulls, tie them to the boat with long strings, and make them fly as we want them, how capital it would be!'

'Or bore a hole through a shark's tail, and reeve a rope through it, eh?' remarked Jack. 'But, I say, it seems that my wish is going to be granted, for here comes a breeze. Ship your oar, Peterkin. Up with the mast, Ralph; I'll see to the sail. Mind your helm; look out for squalls!'

This last speech was caused by the sudden appearance of a dark blue line on the horizon, which swept down on us, lashing up the sea in white foam as it went. We presented the stern of the boat to its first violence, and, in a few seconds, it moderated into a steady breeze, to which we spread our sail and flew merrily over the waves. Although the breeze died away soon afterwards, it had been so stiff while it lasted, that we were carried over the greater part of our way before it fell calm again; so that, when the flapping of the sail against the mast told us that it was time to resume the oars, we were not much more than a mile from Penguin Island.

'There go the soldiers!' cried Peterkin, as we came in sight of it. 'How spruce their white trousers look this morning! I wonder if they will receive us kindly. D' you think they are hospitable, Jack?'

'Don't talk, Peterkin, but pull away, and you shall see shortly.'

As we drew near to the island we were much amused by the appearance of these strange birds. They seemed to be of different species, for some had crests on their heads while others had none, and while some were about the size of a goose others appeared nearly as large as a swan. We also saw a huge albatross soaring above the heads of the penguins. It was followed and surrounded by numerous flocks of sea-gulls.

Having approached to within a few yards of the island, which was a low rock, with no other vegetation on it than a few bushes, we lay on our oars and gazed at the birds with surprise and pleasure, they returning our gaze with interest. We now saw that their soldier-like appearance was owing to the stiff, erect manner in which they sat on their short legs – 'Bolt upright,' as Peterkin expressed it. They had black heads, long sharp beaks, white breasts, and bluish backs. Their wings were so short that they looked more like the fins of a fish, and, indeed, we soon saw that they used them for the purpose of swimming under water. There were no quills on these wings, but a sort of scaly feathers; which also thickly covered their bodies. Their legs were placed so far back that the birds, while on land, were obliged to stand quite upright in order to keep their balance; but in the water they floated like other water-fowl. At first we were so stunned with the clamour which they and other sea-birds kept up around us, that we knew not which way to look – for they covered the rocks in thousands; but, as we continued to gaze, we observed several quadrupeds (as we thought) walking in the midst of the penguins.

'Pull in a bit,' cried Peterkin, 'and let's see what these are. They must be fond of noisy company, to consort with such creatures.'

To our surprise we found that these were no other than penguins which had gone down on all fours, and were crawling among the bushes on their feet and wings, just like quadrupeds. Suddenly one big old bird became alarmed, and, scuttling down the rocks, plumped or fell, rather than ran, into the sea. It dived in a moment, and, a few seconds afterwards, came out of the water far ahead, with such a spring, and such a dive back into the sea again, that we could scarcely believe it was not a fish that had leaped in sport.

'That beats everything,' said Peterkin. 'I've heard of a thing being neither fish, flesh, nor fowl, but I never did expect to live to see a brute that was all three together – at once – in one! But look there!' he continued, pointing with a look of resignation to the shore. 'Look there! There's no end to it. What *has* that brute got under its tail?'

We turned to look, and saw a penguin walking slowly and very sedately along the shore with an egg under its tail. There were several others, we observed, burdened in the same way; and we found afterwards that these were a species of penguins that always carried their eggs so. Indeed, they had a most convenient cavity for the purpose, just between the tail and the legs. We were much impressed with the regularity and order of this colony. The island seemed to be apportioned out into squares, of which each penguin possessed one, and sat in stiff solemnity in the middle of it, or took a slow march up and down the spaces between. Some were hatching their eggs, but others were feeding their young ones in a manner that caused us to laugh not a little. The mother stood on a mound or raised rock, while the young one stood patiently below her on the ground. Suddenly the mother raised her head and uttered a series of the most discordant cackling sounds.

'She's going to choke,' cried Peterkin.

But this was not the case, although, I confess, she looked like it. In a few seconds she put down her head and opened her mouth, into which the young one thrust its beak and seemed to suck something from her throat. Then the cackling was renewed, the suckling continued, and so the operation of feeding was carried on till the young one was satisfied.

'Now, just look yonder!' said Peterkin, in an excited tone. 'If that isn't the most abominable piece of maternal deception I ever saw. That rascally old lady penguin has just pitched her young one into the sea, and there's another about to follow her example.'

This indeed seemed to be the case, for, on the top of a steep rock close to the edge of the sea, we observed an old penguin endeavouring to entice her young one into the water; but the young one seemed very unwilling to go. At last she went gently behind the young bird and pushed it a little towards the water, but no sooner did she get it to the edge of the rock than she gave it a sudden and violent push, sending it head-long down the slope into the water, where its mother left it to scramble ashore as it best could. We came to the conclusion that this is the way in which old penguins teach their children to swim.

Scarcely had we finished making our remarks on this, when we were startled by about a dozen of the old birds hopping in the most clumsy and ludicrous manner towards the sea. The instant they reached the water, however, they seemed to be in their proper element. They dived and bounded out of it and into it again with the utmost agility; and so, diving and bounding and spluttering, for they could not fly, they went rapidly out to sea.

'I vote for landing, so pull in, lads,' said Jack. In a few seconds we ran the boat into a little creek, where we made her fast to a projecting piece of coral, and, running up the beach, entered the ranks of the penguins armed with our cudgels and our spear. We were greatly surprised to find that, instead of attacking us or showing signs of fear at our approach, these curious birds did not move from their places until we laid hands on them, and merely turned their eyes on us in solemn, stupid wonder as we passed.

We spent fully three hours on this island in watching the habits of these curious birds, and, when we finally left them, we all three concluded that they were the most wonderful creatures in the world!

It was evening before we left the island of the penguins. As we had made up our minds to camp for the night on a small island about two miles off, whereon grew a few coconut trees, we lay to our oars with some energy. But a danger was in store for us which we had not anticipated. The wind, which had carried us so quickly to Penguin Island, freshened as evening drew on to a stiff breeze, and, before we had made half the distance to the small island, it became a regular gale. Although it was not so directly against us as to prevent our rowing in the course we wished to go, yet it checked us very much. The waves soon began to rise, and to roll their broken crests against our small craft, so that she began to take in water, and we had much ado to keep ourselves afloat. At last the wind and sea together became so violent that we found it impossible to make the island, so Jack suddenly put the head of the boat round and ordered Peterkin and me to hoist a corner of the sail, intending to run back to Penguin Island.

'We shall at least have the shelter of the bushes,' he said, as the boat flew before the wind, 'and the penguins will keep us company.'

As Jack spoke, the wind suddenly shifted, and blew so much against us that we were forced to hoist more of the sail in order to beat up for the island, being by this change thrown much to leeward of it. What made matters worse was, that the gale came in squalls, so that we were more than once nearly upset.

'Stand by, both of you,' cried Jack, in a quick, earnest tone; 'be ready to dowse the sail. I very much fear we won't make the island after all.'

Peterkin and I were so much in the habit of trusting everything to Jack that we had fallen into the way of not considering things as were under Jack's care. We had, therefore, never doubted for a moment that all was going well. However, we had no time for question or surmise, for a heavy squall was bearing down upon us, and, as we were then flying with our lee gunwale dipping occasionally under the waves, it was evident that we should have to lower our sail altogether. In a few seconds the squall struck the boat, but Peterkin and I had the sail down in a moment, so that it did not upset us; but, when it was past, we were more than half full of water. This I soon baled out, while Peterkin again hoisted a corner of the sail; but the evil which Jack had feared came upon us. We found it quite impossible to make Penguin Island. The gale carried us quickly past it towards the open sea, and the terrible truth flashed upon us that we should be swept out and left to perish miserably in a small boat in the midst of the wide ocean.

We trembled as we gazed around us, for we were now beyond the shelter of the islands, and it seemed as though any of the huge billows, which curled over in masses of foam, might swallow us up in a moment. The water, also, began to wash in over our sides, and I had to keep constantly baling, for Jack could not quit the helm nor Peterkin the sail for an instant, without endangering our lives. In the midst of this distress Jack uttered an exclamation of hope, and pointed towards a low island or rock which lay directly ahead.

As we neared this rock we observed that it was quite destitute of trees and verdure, and so low that the sea broke completely over it. In fact, it was nothing more than the summit of one of the coral formations, which rose only a few feet above the level of the water. Over this island the waves were breaking in the utmost fury, and our hearts sank within us as we saw that there was not a spot where we could thrust our little boat without its being dashed to pieces.

'Show a little bit more sail,' cried Jack, as we swept past the weather side of the rock with fearful speed.

'Ay, ay,' answered Peterkin, hoisting about a foot more of our sail.

Little though the addition was, it caused the boat to lie over and creak so loudly, as we cleft the foaming waves, that I expected to be upset every instant; and I blamed Jack in my heart for his rashness. But I did him injustice, for, although the water rushed inboard in a torrent, he succeeded in steering us sharply round to the leeward side of the rock, where the water was comparatively calm, and the force of the breeze broken.

'Out your oars now, lads; that's well done. Give way!' We obeyed instantly. The oars splashed into the waves together. One good hearty pull, and we were floating in a comparatively calm creek that was so narrow as to be barely able to admit our boat. Here we were in perfect safety, and we leaped on shore and fastened our cable to the rocks. We had no lack of food, but we were drenched to the skin; the sea was foaming round us and the spray flying over our heads, so that we were completely enveloped, as it were, in water; the spot on which we had landed was not more than twelve yards in diameter, and from this spot we could not move without the risk of being swept away by the storm. At the upper end of the creek was a small hollow or cave in the rock, which sheltered us from the fury of the winds and waves.

'Now, boys,' cried Jack, 'bestir yourselves, and let's make ourselves comfortable. Toss out our provisions, Peterkin; and here, Ralph, lend a hand to haul up the boat. Look sharp.'

'Ay, ay, captain,' we cried, as we hastened to obey, much cheered by the hearty manner of our comrade.

Fortunately the cave, although not very deep, was quite dry, so that we succeeded in making ourselves comfortable. We landed our provisions, wrung the water out of our garments, spread our sail below us for a carpet, and, after having eaten a hearty meal, began to feel quite cheerful. But as night drew on, our spirits sank again. We were stunned with the violence of the tempest that raged around us. The night grew pitchy dark, so that we could not see our hands when we held them up before our eyes. The storm at last became so terrible that it was difficult to make our voices audible. A slight variation of the wind caused a few drops of spray ever and anon to blow into our faces; and the eddy of the sea, in its mad boiling, washed up into our little creek until it reached our feet and threatened to tear away our boat. In order to prevent this latter calamity, we hauled the boat farther up and held the cable in our hands. Occasional flashes of lightning shone with a ghastly glare through the watery curtains around us, and lent additional horror to the scene. Yet we longed for those dismal flashes, for they were less appalling than the thick blackness that succeeded them. Crashing peals of thunder fell upon our ears through the wild yelling of the hurricane.

For three days and three nights we remained on this rock, while the storm continued to rage with unabated fury. On the morning of the fourth day it suddenly ceased, and the wind fell altogether; but the waves still ran so high that we did not dare to put off in our boat. During the greater part of this period we scarcely slept above a few minutes at a time, but on the third night we slept soundly and awoke early on the fourth morning to find the sea very much down, and the sun shining brightly.

It was with light hearts that we launched forth once more in our little boat and steered away for our island home. As it was a dead calm we had to row during the greater part of the day; but towards the afternoon a fair breeze sprang up, which enabled us to hoist our sail. We soon passed Penguin Island, but as we were anxious to get home, we did not land, to the great disappointment of Peterkin, who seemed to entertain quite an affection for the penguins.

Although the breeze was pretty fresh for several hours, we did not reach the outer reef of our island till nightfall, and before we had sailed more than a hundred yards into the lagoon, the wind died away altogether, so that we had to take to our oars again. It was late and the moon and stars were shining brightly when we arrived opposite the bower and leaped upon the strand. So glad were we to be safe back again on our beloved island, that we scarcely took time to drag the boat a short way up the beach, and then ran up to see that all was right at the bower. On reaching it we found everything just as it had been left, and the black cat curled up, sound asleep, on the coral table.

CHAPTER IX

For many months after this we continued to live on our island in uninterrupted harmony. Sometimes we went out fishing in the lagoon, and sometimes went hunting in the woods, or ascended to the mountain-top, by way of variety, although Peterkin always asserted that we went for the purpose of hailing any ship that might chance to heave in sight. But I am certain that none of us wished to be delivered from our captivity, for we were extremely happy, and Peterkin used to say that as we were very young we should not feel the loss of a year or two. Peterkin was fourteen years of age, Jack eighteen, and I fifteen. But Jack was very tall, strong and manly for his age, and might easily have been mistaken for twenty.

The climate was so beautiful that it seemed to be a per-petual summer, and as many of the fruit trees continued to bear fruit and blossom all the year round, we never wanted for a plentiful supply of food. The hogs, too, seemed rather to increase than diminish, although Peterkin was very frequent in his attacks on them with his spear.

We employed ourselves very busily during this time in making various garments of coconut cloth, as those with which we had landed were beginning to be very ragged. Peterkin also succeeded in making excellent shoes out of the skin of the old hog, in the following manner: he first cut a piece of the hide, of an oblong form, a few inches longer than his foot. This he soaked in water, and, while it was wet, he sewed up one end of it, so as to form a rough imitation of that part of the heel of a shoe where the seam is. This done, he bored a row of holes all round the edge of the piece of skin, through which a tough line was passed. Into the sewed-up part of this shoe he thrust his heel, then, drawing the string tight, the edges rose up and overlapped his foot all round. It is true there were a great many ill-looking puckers in these shoes, but we found them very serviceable notwithstanding, and Jack came at last to prefer them to his long boots.

Diving in the Water Garden continued to afford us as much pleasure as ever; and Peterkin began to be a little more expert in the water from constant practice. As for Jack and me, we began to feel as if water were our native element.

Now while we were engaged with these occupations and amusements, an event occurred one day which was as unexpected as it was exceedingly alarming and very horrible.

Jack and I were sitting on the rocks at Spouting Cliff, and Peterkin was wringing the water from his garments, having recently fallen by accident into the sea – a thing he was constantly doing – when our attention was suddenly arrested by two objects which appeared on the horizon.

'What are yon, think you?' I said, addressing Jack.

'I can't imagine,' answered he. 'I've noticed them for some time, and fancied they were black sea-gulls, but the more I look at them the more I feel convinced they are much larger than gulls.'

'They seem to be coming towards us,' said I.

'Hallo! what's wrong?' enquired Peterkin, coming up.

'Look there,' said Jack.

'Whales!' cried Peterkin, shading his eyes with his hands. 'No! eh! *can* they be boats, Jack?'

Our hearts beat with excitement at the very thought of seeing human faces again.

'I think you are about right, Peterkin; but they seem to me to move strangely for boats,' said Jack.

I noticed that a shade of anxiety crossed Jack's countenance as he gazed long and intently at the two objects, which were now nearing us fast. At last he sprang to his feet. 'They are canoes, Ralph! Whether war-canoes or not I cannot tell, but this I know, that all the natives of the South Sea Islands are fierce cannibals, and they have little respect for strangers. We must hide if they land here, which I earnestly hope they will not do.'

I was greatly alarmed at Jack's speech, and it was with very uncomfortable feelings that Peterkin and I followed him quickly into the woods.

'How unfortunate,' said I, as we gained the shelter of the bushes, 'that we have forgotten our arms.'

'It matters not,' said Jack; 'here are clubs enough and to spare.' As he spoke, he laid his hand on a bundle of stout poles of various sizes, which Peterkin's ever-busy hands had formed.

We each selected a stout club and lay down behind a rock, whence we could see the canoes approach, without ourselves being seen. At first we made an occasional remark on their appearance, but after they entered the lagoon, and drew near the beach, we ceased to speak, and gazed with intense interest at the scene before us.

We now observed that the foremost canoe was being chased by the other, and that it contained a few women and children, as well as men – perhaps forty souls altogether; while the canoe which pursued it contained only men. They seemed to be about the same in number, but were better armed, and looked like a war party. Both crews were paddling with all their might. The foremost canoe made for the beach close beneath the rocks behind which we were concealed. Their short paddles flashed in the water, and sent up a constant shower of spray. The foam curled from the prow, and the eyes of the rowers glistened in their black faces as they strained every muscle of their naked bodies; nor did they relax their efforts till the canoe struck the beach with a violent shock; then the whole party sprang from the canoe to the shore. Three women, two of whom carried infants, rushed into the woods; and the men crowded to the water's edge, with stones in their hands, spears levelled, and clubs brandished, to resist the landing of their enemies.

The pursuers neared the shore; they came like a wild charger. The canoe struck, and, with a yell they leaped into the water, and drove their enemies up the beach.

The battle that followed was frightful to behold. Most of the men wielded clubs of enormous size and curious shapes, with which they dashed out each other's brains. As they were almost entirely naked, they looked more like demons than human beings. I felt my heart grow sick at the sight of this bloody battle, and would fain have turned away, but a species of fascination seemed to glue my eyes upon the combatants. The attacking party was led by a most extraordinary being, who, from his size and peculiarity, I concluded was a chief. His hair was frizzed out so that it resembled a large turban. It was of a light-yellow hue, which surprised me much, for the man's body was as black as coal, and I felt convinced that the hair must have been dyed. He was tattooed from head to foot; and his face, besides being tattooed, was besmeared with red paint, and streaked with white. Altogether, with his yellow turban-like hair, his Herculean black frame, his glittering eyes and white teeth, he seemed the most terrible monster I ever beheld. He was very active in the fight, and had already killed four men.

Suddenly the yellow-haired chief was attacked by a man quite as strong and large as himself. He flourished a heavy club something like an eagle's beak at the point. For a second or two these giants eyed each other warily, moving round and round, as if to catch each other at a disadvantage, but seeing that nothing was to be gained by this caution, they apparently made up their minds to attack at the same instant, for, with a wild shout and simultaneous spring, they swung their heavy clubs. Suddenly the yellow-haired savage tripped, his enemy sprang forward, the ponderous club was swung, but it did not descend, for at that moment the savage was felled to the ground by a stone from the hand of one who had witnessed his chief's danger. This was the turning-point in the battle. The savages who landed first turned and fled towards the bush, on seeing the fall of their chief. But not one escaped. They were all overtaken and felled to the earth. I saw, however, that they were not all killed. Indeed, their enemies, now that they were conquered, seemed anxious to take them alive; and they succeeded in securing fifteen, whom they bound hand and foot with cords, and, carrying them up into the woods, laid them down among the bushes. Here they left them, and returned to the scene of the late battle, where the remnant of the party were bathing their wounds.

Out of the forty blacks that composed the attacking party, only twenty-eight remained alive, two of whom were sent into the bush to hunt for the women and children. Of the other party, as I have said, only fifteen survived, and these were lying bound and helpless.

Jack and Peterkin and I looked at each other, and whispered our fears that the savages might clamber up the rocks to search for fresh water, and so discover our place of concealment; but we agreed to remain where we were; and, indeed, we could not easily have risen without exposing ourselves to detection. One of the savages now went up to the wood and soon returned with a bundle of firewood, and we were not a little surprised to see him set fire to it by the very same means used by Jack the time we made our first fire – namely, with the bow and drill. When the fire was kindled, two of the pary went again to the woods and returned with one of the bound men. A dreadful feeling of horror crept over my heart, as the thought flashed upon me that they were going to burn their enemies. As they bore him to the fire my feelings almost overpowered me. I gasped for breath, and seizing my club, endeavoured to spring to my feet; but Jack's powerful arm pinned me to the earth. Next moment one of the savages raised his club, and fractured the wretched creature's skull. He must have died instantly, and, strange though it may seem, I confess to a feeling of relief when the deed was done, because I now knew that the poor man could not be burned alive. Scarcely had his limbs ceased to quiver when the monsters cut slices from his body, and, after roasting them slightly over the fire, devoured them.

Suddenly there arose a cry from the woods, and, in a few

seconds, the two savages hastened towards the fire dragging the three women and their two infants along with them. One of those women was much younger than her companions and we were struck with the gentle expression of her face, which, although she had the flattish nose and thick lips of the others, was of a light-brown colour, and we conjectured that she must be of a different race. She and her companions wore short petticoats and a kind of tippet on their shoulders. Their hair was jet black, but instead of being long, was short and curly – though not woolly. While we gazed with interest and some anxiety at these poor creatures, the big chief advanced to one of the elder females and laid his hand upon the child. But the mother shrank from him, and clasping the little one to her bosom, uttered a wail of fear. With a savage laugh, the chief tore the child from her arms and tossed it into the sea. A low groan burst from Jack's lips as we witnessed this atrocious act and heard the mother's shriek, as she fell insensible on the sand. The rippling waves rolled the child on the beach and we could observe that the little one still lived.

The young girl was now brought forward, and the chief addressed her; but although we heard his voice, and even the words distinctly, of course we could not understand what he said. The girl made no answer to his fierce questions, and we saw by the way in which he pointed to the fire that he threatened her life.

'Peterkin,' said Jack in a hoarse whisper, 'have you got your knife?'

'Yes,' replied Peterkin, whose face was pale as death.

'That will do. Listen to me, and do my bidding quick. Here is the small knife, Ralph. Fly both of you through the bush, cut the cords that bind the prisoners and set them free. Quick, ere it be too late.' Jack sprang up, and seized a heavy but short bludgeon.

At this moment the man who had butchered the native a few minutes before advanced towards the girl with his heavy club. Jack uttered a yell that rang like a death shriek among the rocks. With one bound he leaped over a precipice full fifteen feet high, and, before the men had recovered from their surprise, was in the midst of them; while Peterkin and I dashed through the bushes towards the prisoners. With one blow of his staff Jack felled the man with the club, then, turning round with a look of fury, he rushed upon the big chief with the yellow hair. Had the blow which Jack aimed at his head taken effect, the huge savage would have needed no second stroke; but he was agile as a cat, and avoided it by springing to one side, while, at the same time, he swung his ponderous club at the head of his foe. It was now Jack's turn to leap aside. He was cool now. He darted his blows rapidly and well, and the superiority of his light weapon was strikingly proved in this combat, for while he could easily evade the blows of the chief's heavy club, the chief could not so easily evade those of the light one.

It was lucky for Jack that the other blacks considered the success of their chief in this encounter to be so certain that they refrained from interfering. They contented themselves with awaiting the issue.

The force which the chief expended in wielding his club now began to be apparent. His movements became slower, his breath hissed through his clenched teeth, and the surprised natives drew nearer in order to render assistance. Jack observed this movement. He felt that his fate was sealed, and resolved to cast his life upon the next blow. The chief's club was again about to descend on his head. He might have evaded it easily, but instead of doing so, he suddenly shortened his grasp of his own club, rushed in under the blow, struck his adversary right between the eyes with all his force, and fell to the earth, crushed beneath the senseless body of the chief. A dozen clubs flew high in air ready to descend on the head of Jack, but they hesitated a moment for the massive body of the chief completely covered him. That moment saved his life. Before the natives could tear the chief's body away, seven of their number fell prostrate beneath the clubs of the prisoners whom Peterkin and I had set free, and two others fell under our own hand. We could never have accomplished this had not our enemies been so engrossed with the fight between Jack and their chief that they had failed to observe us until we were upon them. They still outnumbered our party by three, but we were flushed with victory while they were taken by surprise and dispirited by the fall of their chief. Moreover, they were awestruck by the sweeping fury of Jack, who seemed to have lost his senses altogether, and had no sooner shaken himself free of the chief's body than he rushed into the midst of them, and in three blows equalized our numbers. Peterkin and I flew to the rescue, the natives followed us, and, in less than ten minutes our opponents were knocked down or made prisoners, bound hand and foot, and extended side by side upon the seashore.

After the battle was over, the blacks crowded round us, while they continued to pour upon us a flood of questions, which of course we could not answer. Jack took the chief (who had recovered from the effects of his wound) by the hand and shook it warmly. No sooner did the blacks see that this was meant to express goodwill than they shook hands with us all round. After this ceremony Jack went up to the girl, who had never once moved from the rock where she had been left. He made signs to her to follow him, and then, taking the chief by the hand, was about to conduct him to the bower, when his eye fell on the poor infant which had been thrown into the sea and was still lying on the shore. He hastened towards it, and, to his great joy, found it to be still alive. We also found that the mother was beginning to recover slowly.

'Here, get out o' the way,' said Jack, pushing us aside, as we stooped over the poor woman and endeavoured to restore her, 'I'll soon bring her round.' So saying, he placed the infant on her bosom and laid its warm cheek on hers. The effect was wonderful. The woman opened her eyes, felt the child, looked at it, and with a cry of joy clasped it in her arms.

'There, that's all right,' said Jack, once more taking the chief by the hand. 'Now, Ralph and Peterkin, make the women and these fellows follow me to the bower. We'll entertain them as hospitably as we can.'

In a few minutes the blacks were all seated on the ground in front of the bower making a hearty meal off a cold roast pig, several ducks, and a variety of cold fish, together with an unlimited supply of coconuts, bread-fruit, yams, taro, and plums.

Meanwhile, we three, being thoroughly knocked up with out day's work, took a good draught of coconut lemonade, and throwing ourselves on our beds fell fast asleep. The natives followed our example, and in half an hour the whole camp was buried in repose.

How long we slept I cannot tell, but when we lay down the sun was setting and when we awoke it was high in the heavens. I awoke Jack, who started up in surprise, being unable at first to comprehend our situation. 'Now, then,' said he, springing up, 'let's see after breakfast. Hallo! Peterkin, lazy fellow, how long do you mean to lie there?'

Peterkin yawned heavily. 'Well!' said he, opening his eyes and looking up after some trouble, 'if it isn't tomorrow morning, and me thinking it was today all this time. Hallo! Venus, where did you come from? You seem tolerably at home, anyhow.'

This remark was called forth by the sight of one of the females, who had seated herself on the rock in front of the bower, and, having placed her child at her feet, was busily engaged in devouring the remains of a roast pig.

By this time the natives outside were all astir, and breakfast in an advanced state of preparation. During the course of it we made sundry attempts to converse with the natives by signs, but without effect. At last we hit upon a plan of discovering their names. Jack pointed to his breast and said 'Jack,' very distinctly; then he pointed to Peterkin and to me, repeating our names at the same time. Then he pointed to himself again, and said 'Jack,' and laying his finger on the breast of the chief, looked inquiringly into his face. The chief instantly understood him and said 'Tararo,' twice, distinctly. Jack repeated it after him. Then turning towards the youngest of the women, who was seated at the door of the bower, he pointed to her; whereupon the chief said, 'Avatea'; and pointing towards the sun, raised his finger slowly towards the zenith, where it remained steadily for a minute or two.

'What can that mean, I wonder,' said Jack, looking puzzled.

'Perhaps,' said Peterkin, 'the chief means she is an angel come down to stay here for a while. If so, she's an uncommonly black one!'

We did not feel quite satisfied with this explanation, so Jack went up to her and said: 'Avatea.' The woman smiled sadly, and nodded her head, at the same time pointing to her breast and then to the sun, in the same manner as the chief had done. We were much puzzled to know what this could signify.

Jack now made signs to the natives to follow him, and, taking up his axe, he led them to the place where the battle had been fought. Here we found the prisoners, who had passed the night on the beach. They did not seem the worse for their exposure, however, as we judged by the hearty appetite with which they devoured the breakfast given to them. Jack then began to dig a hole in the sand, and, after working a few seconds, he pointed to it and to the dead bodies that lay on the beach. The natives immediately perceived what he wanted, and, running for their paddles, dug a hole in the course of half an hour that was quite large enough to contain all the bodies of the slain. When it was finished they tossed their dead enemies into it with so much indifference that we felt assured they would not have put themselves to this trouble had we not asked them to do so. The body of the yellow-haired chief was the last thrown in.

While they were about to throw the sand over this chief, one of the savages stooped over him, and with a knife, made apparently of stone, cut a large slice of flesh from his thigh. We knew at once that he intended to make use of this for food, and could not repress a cry of horror and disgust.

'Come, come, you blackguard,' cried Jack, starting up and seizing the man by the arm, 'pitch that into the hole. Do you hear?'

The savage of course did not understand the command, but he perfectly understood the look of disgust with which Jack regarded the flesh, and his fierce gaze as he pointed towards the hole. Nevertheless he did not obey. Jack instantly turned to Tararo and made signs to him to enforce obedience. The chief seemed to understand the appeal, for he stepped forward, raised his club, and was on the point of dashing out the brains of his offending subject, when Jack sprang forward and caught his uplifted arm.

'Stop!' he shouted. 'You blockhead, I don't want you to kill the man.' He then pointed again to the flesh and to the hole. The chief uttered a few words, which had the desired effect; for the man threw the flesh into the hole, which was immediately filled up. This man was of a morose, sulky disposition, and, during all the time he remained on the island, regarded us, especially Jack, with a scowling visage. His name, we found, was Mahine.

The next three or four days were spent by the natives in mending their canoe, which had been damaged by the violent shock it had sustained on striking the shore. This canoe was a very curious structure. It was about thirty feet long, and had a high towering stern. The timbers were fastened much in the same way as those of our little boat were put together; but the part that seemed most curious to us was a sort of out-rigger, or long plank, which was attached to the body of the canoe by means of two stout cross-beams. These beams kept the plank parallel with the canoe, but not in contact with it, for it floated in the water with an open space between; thus forming a sort of double canoe. This we found was intended to prevent the upsetting of the canoe.

When the canoe was ready, we assisted the natives to carry the prisoners into it, and helped them to load it with provisions and fruit. Peterkin also went to the plum tree for the purpose of making a special onslaught upon the hogs, and killed no less than six of them. These we baked and presented to our friends on the day of their departure. On that day Tararo made a great many energetic signs to us, which, after much consideration, we came to understand were proposals that we should go away with him to his island; but we shook our heads very decidedly. However, we consoled him by presenting him with our rusty axe. We also gave him a piece of wood with our names carved on it, and a piece of string to hang it round his neck as an ornament.

In a few minutes more we were all assembled on the beach. Being unable to speak to the blacks, we went through the ceremony of shaking hands, and expected they would depart; but, before doing so, Tararo went up to Jack and rubbed noses with him, after which he did the same with Peterkin and me! Seeing that this was their mode of salutation, we determined to conform to their custom, so we rubbed noses heartily with the whole party, women and all! Avatea was the last to take leave of us, and we experienced a feeling of real sorrow when she approached to bid us farewell. Going up to Jack, she put out her flat nose to be rubbed, and thereafter paid the same compliment to Peterkin and me.

An hour later the canoe was out of sight, and we were seated in silence beneath the shadow of our bower, meditating on the events of the last few days.

CHAPTER X

After these poor blacks had left us, we used to hold long and frequent conversations about them, and I noticed that Peterkin's manner was now much altered. Often there was a tone of deep seriousness in his manner, which made him seem to Jack and me as if he had grown two years older within a few days.

One day we were all enjoying ourselves in the Water Garden, preparatory to going on a fishing excursion. Peterkin was sunning himself on the ledge of rock, while we were creeping among the rocks below. Happening to look up, I observed Peterkin making violent gesticulation for us to come up; so I gave Jack a push, and rose immediately.

'A sail! a sail! Ralph, look! Jack, away on the horizon there, just over the entrance to the lagoon!' cried Peterkin, as we scrambled up the rocks.

'So it is, and a schooner, too!' said Jack, as he proceeded hastily to dress.

Our hearts were thrown into a terrible flutter by this discovery, for if it should touch at our island we had no doubt the captain would be happy to give us a passage to some of the civilized islands, where we could find a ship sailing for England, or some other part of Europe. Home, with all its associations, rushed in upon my heart like a flood. With joyful anticipations we hastened to the highest point of rock near our dwelling, and awaited the arrival of the vessel, for we now perceived that she was making straight for the island, under a steady breeze.

In less than an hour she was close to the reef, where she rounded to, and backed her topsails in order to survey the coast. Seeing this, and fearing that they might not perceive us, we all three waved pieces of coconut cloth in the air, and soon had the satisfaction of seeing them beginning to lower a boat and bustle about the decks as if they meant to land. Suddenly a flag was run up to the peak, a little cloud of white smoke rose from the schooner's side, and, before we could guess their intentions, a cannon shot came crashing through the bushes, carried away several coconut trees in its passage, and burst against the cliff a few yards below the spot on which we stood.

With feelings of terror we now observed that the flag at the schooner's peak was black, with a death's head and cross-bones upon it. As we gazed at each other in blank amazement, the word 'pirate' escaped our lips simultaneously.

'What is to be done?' cried Peterkin, as we observed a boat shoot from the vessel's side, and make for the entrance of the reef. 'If they take us off the island, it will either be to throw us overboard for sport, or to make pirates of us.'

Jack stood with folded arms, and his eyes fixed with a grave, anxious expression on the ground. 'There is but one hope,' said he, turning with a sad expression of countenance to Peterkin; 'perhaps, after all, we may not have to resort to it. If these villains are anxious to take us, they will soon overrun the whole island. But come, follow me.'

Jack bounded into the woods, and led us by a circuitous route to Spouting Cliff. Here he halted, and, advancing cautiously to the rocks, glanced over their edge. We were soon by his side, and saw the boat, which was crowded with armed men, just touching the shore. In an instant the crew landed, formed line, and rushed up to our bower.

In a few seconds we saw them hurrying back to the boat, one of them swinging the poor cat round his head by the tail. On reaching the water's edge, he tossed it far into the sea, and joined his companions, who appeared to be holding a hasty council.

'You see what we may expect,' said Jack, bitterly. 'Now, boys, we have but one chance left – the Diamond Cave.'

'The Diamond Cave!' cried Peterkin. 'Then my chance is a

poor one, for I could not dive into it if all the pirates on the Pacific were at my heels.'

'Nay, but,' said I, 'we will take you down, Peterkin, if you will only trust us.'

As I spoke, we observed the pirates scatter over the beach, and radiate towards the woods and along shore.

'Now, Peterkin,' said Jack, in a solemn tone, 'you must make up your mind to do it, or we must make up our minds to die in your company.'

'There are five of them,' said I; 'we have no chance.'

'Come, then,' cried Peterkin, 'let us dive; I will go.'

Those who are not naturally expert in the water will understand the amount of resolution that it required in Peterkin to allow himself to be dragged down to a depth of ten feet, and then, through a narrow tunnel, into an almost pitch-dark cavern. But there was no alternative. The pirates had already caught sight of us, and were now within a short distance of the rocks.

Jack and I seized Peterkin by the arms.

'Now, keep quite still, no struggling,' said Jack, 'or we are lost.'

Peterkin made no reply, but the stern gravity of his marble features satisfied us that he had fully made up his mind to go through with it. Just as the pirates gained the foot of the rocks, which hid us for a moment from their view, we bent over the sea, and plunged down together head foremost. Peterkin behaved like a hero. He floated passively between us like a log of wood, and we passed the tunnel and rose into the cave in a shorter space of time than I had ever done it before.

Peterkin drew a long, deep breath on reaching the surface; and in a few seconds we were all standing on the ledge of rock in safety. Jack now searched for the tinder and torch, which always lay in the cave. He soon found them, and, lighting the torch, revealed to Peterkin's wondering gaze the marvels of the place. But we were too wet to waste much time in looking about us. Our first care was to take off our clothes, and wring them as dry as we could. This done, we proceeded to examine the state of our larder, for there was no knowing how long the pirates might remain on the island.

'Perhaps,' said Peterkin, 'they may take it into their heads to stop here altogether, and so we shall be buried alive in this place.'

'Don't you think, Peterkin, that it's the nearest thing to being drowned alive that you ever felt?' said Jack with a smile. 'But I've no fear of that. These villains never stay long on shore. The sea is their home, so you may depend upon it that they won't stay more than a day or two.'

We now began to make arrangements for spending the night in the cavern. At various periods Jack and I had conveyed coconuts and other fruits, besides rolls of coconut cloth, to this submarine cave, partly for amusement, and partly from a feeling that we might possibly be driven one day to take shelter here from the natives. Little did we imagine that the first savages who would drive us into it would be white savages, perhaps our own countrymen. We found the coconuts in good condition, and the cooked yams, but the bread-fruits were spoiled. We also found the cloth where we had left it; and, on opening it out, there proved to be sufficient to make a bed; which was important as the rock was damp. Having collected it all together, we spread out our bed, placed our torch in the midst of us, and ate our supper. It was indeed a strange chamber to feast in; and we could not help remarking on the cold ghastly appearance of the walls, and the black water at our side, with the thick darkness beyond.

We sat long over our meal, talking together in subdued voices, for we did not like the dismal echoes that rang through the vault above when we happened to raise them. At last the faint light that came through the opening died away, warning us that it was night and time for rest. We therefore put out our torch and lay down to sleep.

On awaking, it was some time before we could remember where we were, and we were in much uncertainty as to whether it was early or late. We saw by the faint light that it was day, but could not guess at the hour; so Jack proposed that he should dive out and reconnoitre.

'No, Jack,' said I, 'do you rest here. You've had enough to do during the last few days. Rest yourself now, while I go out to see what the pirates are about. I'll be very careful not to expose myself, and I'll bring you word again in a short time.'

'Very well, Ralph,' answered Jack, 'please yourself, but don't be long; and if you'll take my advice you'll go in your clothes, for I would like to have some fresh coconuts, and climbing trees without clothes is uncomfortable, to say the least of it.'

'The pirates will be sure to keep a sharp look-out,' said Peterkin, 'so be careful.'

'No fear,' said I. 'Goodbye.'

'Goodbye,' answered my comrades.

And while the words were yet sounding in my ears, I plunged into the water, and in a few seconds found myself in the open air. On rising, I was careful to come up gently and to breathe softly, while I kept close in beside the rocks; but, as I observed no one near me, I crept slowly out, and ascended the cliff a step at a time, till I obtained a full view of the shore. No pirates were to be seen – even their boat was gone; but as it was possible they might have hidden themselves, I did not venture too boldly forward. Then it occurred to me to look out to sea, when, to my surprise, I saw the pirate schooner sailing away almost hull down on the horizon! On seeing this I uttered a shout of joy. Then ran to the top of the cliff, to make sure that the vessel I saw was indeed the pirate schooner. I looked long and anxiously at her, and said aloud: 'Yes, there she goes; the villains have been baulked of their prey this time at least.'

'Not so sure of that!' said a deep voice at my side; while a heavy hand grasped my shoulder.

My heart seemed to leap into my throat at the words; and, turning round, I beheld a man of immense stature and fierce aspect regarding me with a smile of contempt. He was a white man – that is to say, he was a man of European blood, though his face, from long exposure to the weather, was deeply bronzed. His dress was that of a common seaman, except that he had on a Greek skull-cap, and wore a broad shawl of the richest silk round his waist. In this shawl were placed two pair of pistols and a heavy cutlass. He wore a beard and moustache, which, like the locks on his head, were short, curly, and sprinkled with grey hairs.

'So, youngster,' he said, while I felt his grasp tighten on my shoulder, 'the villains have been baulked of their prey, have they? We shall see, we shall see. Now, you whelp, look yonder.' As he spoke, the pirate uttered a shrill whistle. In a second or two it was answered, and the pirate boat rowed round the point at the Water Garden, and came rapidly towards us. 'Now, go, make a fire on that point; and hark'ee, youngster, if you try to run away, I'll send a quick and sure messenger after you,' and he pointed significantly at his pistols.

I obeyed in silence, and as I happened to have the burning-glass in my pocket, a fire was speedily kindled, and a thick smoke ascended into the air. It had scarcely appeared for two minutes when the boom of a gun rolled over the sea, and, looking up, I saw that the schooner was making for the island again. It now flashed across me that this was a ruse on the part of the pirates, and that they had sent their vessel away, knowing that it would lead us to suppose that they had left altogether. I was completely in their power, so I stood helplessly beside the pirate watching the crew of the boat as they landed on the beach.

There was a good deal of jesting at the success of their scheme, as the crew ascended the rocks and addressed the man who had captured me by the title of captain. They were a ferocious set of men, with shaggy beards and scowling brows. All of them were armed with cutlasses and pistols, and their costumes were, with trifling variations, similar to that of the captain. As I looked from one to the other I felt that my life hung by a hair.

'But where are the other cubs?' cried one of the men, with an oath that made me shudder. 'I'll swear to it there were three, at least, if not more.'

'You hear what he says, whelp; where are the other dogs?' said the captain.

'If you mean my companions,' said I, in a low voice, 'I won't tell you.'

A loud laugh burst from the crew at this answer.

The pirate captain looked at me in surprise. Then drawing a pistol from his belt, he cocked it and said: 'Now, youngster, listen to me. I've no time to waste here. If you don't tell me all you know, I'll blow your brains out! Where are your comrades?'

For an instant I hesitated, not knowing what to do in this extremity. Suddenly a thought occurred to me.

'Villain,' said I, shaking my clenched fist in his face, 'if you were to toss me over yonder cliff into the sea, I would not tell you where my companions are, and I dare you to try me!'

The pirate captain grew white with rage as I spoke. 'Say you so?' cried he, uttering a fierce oath. 'Here, lads, take him by the legs and heave him in – quick!'

The men, who were utterly silenced with surprise at my audacity, advanced and seized me, and, as they carried me towards the cliff, I congratulated myself not a little on the success of my scheme, for I knew that once in the water I could rejoin Jack and Peterkin in the cave. But my hopes were suddenly blasted by the captain crying out: 'Hold on, lads, hold on. We'll give him a taste of the thumbscrews before throwing him to the sharks. Away with him into the boat. Look alive! The breeze is freshening.'

The men instantly raised me shoulder high, and hurrying down the rocks, tossed me into the bottom of the boat, where I lay for some time stunned with the violence of my fall.

On recovering sufficiently to raise myself on my elbow, I perceived that we were already outside the coral reef, and close alongside the schooner, which was of small size and clipper built. I had only time to observe this much, when I received a severe kick on the side from one of the men, who ordered me, in a rough voice, to jump aboard. Rising hastily I clambered up the side. In a few minutes the boat was hoisted on deck, the vessel's head put close to the wind, and the Coral Island dropped slowly astern as we beat up against a head sea.

Immediately after coming aboard, the crew were too busily engaged in working the ship and getting in the boat to attend to me, so I remained leaning against the bulwarks close to the gangway, watching their operations. I was surprised to find that there were no guns of any kind in the vessel, which had more of the appearance of a fast-sailing trader than a pirate. But I was struck with the neatness of everything. The brass work of the binnacle and about the tiller were as brightly polished as if they had just come from the foundry. The decks were pure white, and smooth. The masts were clean-scraped and varnished, except at the cross-trees and truck, which were painted black. The standing and running rigging was in the most perfect order, and the sails white as snow. In short, everything evinced an amount of care and strict discipline that would have done credit to a ship of the Royal Navy. There was nothing lumbering about the vessel, excepting, perhaps, a boat, which lay on the deck with its keel up. It seemed disproportionately large for the schooner; but, when I saw that the crew amounted to between thirty and forty men, I concluded that this boat was held in reserve, in case of any accident compelling the crew to desert the vessel.

As I have before said, the costumes of the men were similar to that of the captain. But in head gear they differed not only from him but from each other, some wearing the ordinary straw hat of the merchant service, while others wore cloth caps and red worsted night-caps. I observed that all their arms were sent below, the captain only retaining his cutlass and a single pistol. The captain was the tallest and most powerful man in the ship. He was a lion-like villain; totally devoid of personal fear, and utterly reckless of consequences, and, therefore, a terror to his men, who individually hated him, but unitedly felt it to be their advantage to have him at their head.

But my thoughts soon reverted to the dear companions whom I had left on shore, and as I turned towards the Coral Island, which was now far away to leeward, I sighed deeply, and the tears rolled slowly down my cheeks.

'So you're blubbering, are you, you obstinate whelp?' said the deep voice of the captain, as he came up and gave me a box on the ear that nearly felled me to the deck. 'I don't allow any such weakness aboard o' this ship. So clap a stopper on your eyes or I'll give you something to cry for.'

I flushed with indignation but took out my handkerchief and dried my eyes.

'I thought you were made of better stuff,' continued the captain, angrily; 'I'd rather have a mad bulldog aboard than a water-eyed puppy. But I'll cure you, lad, or introduce you to the sharks before long. Now go below, and stay there till I call you.'

As I walked forward to obey, my eye fell on a small keg standing by the side of the mainmast, on which the word *gunpowder* was written. It immediately flashed across me that, as we were beating up against the wind, anything floating in the sea would be driven on the reef encircling the Coral Island. I also recollected that my old companions had a pistol. Without a moment's hesitation, therefore, I lifted the keg from the deck and tossed it into the sea! An exclamation of surprise burst from the captain and some of the men who witnessed this act of mine.

Striding up to me, and uttering fearful imprecations, the captain raised his hand to strike me, while he shouted: 'Boy! whelp! what mean you by that?'

'If you lower your hand,' said I, in a loud voice, 'I'll tell you. Until you do so I'm dumb!'

The captain stepped back and regarded me with a look of amazement.

'Now,' continued I, 'I threw that keg into the sea because

the wind and waves will carry it to my friends on the Coral Island, who happen to have a pistol, but no powder. I hope that it will reach them soon, and my only regret is that the keg was not a bigger one. Moreover, pirate, you said just now that you thought I was made of better stuff! I'm quite certain of this, that I am made of such stuff as the like of you shall never tame.'

To my surprise the captain smiled, turned on his heel and walked aft, while I went below.

Here, instead of being rudely handled, as I had expected, the men received me with a shout of laughter, and one of them, patting me on the back, said: 'Well done, lad! Bloody Bill, there, was just such a fellow as you are, and he's now the biggest cut-throat of us all.'

'Take a can of beer, lad,' cried another, 'and wet your whistle after that speech o' your'n to the captain.'

I accepted a plate of boiled pork and a yam, which were handed to me by one of the men from the locker on which some of the crew were seated eating their dinner. The zest with which I ate my meal was much abated in consequence of the frightful oaths and the terrible language that flowed from the lips of these godless men, even in the midst of their hilarity and good humour. The man who had been alluded to as Bloody Bill was seated near me, and I could not help wondering at the moody silence he maintained among his comrades. The only difference between him and the others was his taciturnity and his size, for he was nearly, if not quite, as large a man as the captain.

During the remainder of the afternoon I was left to my own reflections, which were anything but agreeable, for I could not banish from my mind the threat about the thumbscrews, of the nature and use of which I had a vague but terrible conception. I was still meditating on my unhappy fate when, just after nightfall, one of the watch on deck called down the hatchway: 'Hallo, there! Send that boy aft to the captain – sharp!'

'Now then, do you hear, youngster? The captain wants

you. Look alive,' said Bloody Bill, raising his huge frame from the locker on which he had been asleep for the last two hours. He sprang up the ladder and I instantly followed him, and, going aft, was shown into the cabin by one of the men.

A small silver lamp which hung from a beam threw a dim soft light over the cabin, which was a small apartment, and comfortably but plainly furnished. Seated on a camp-stool at the table, and busily engaged in examining a chart of the Pacific, was the captain, who looked up as I entered, and, in a quiet voice, bade me be seated, while he threw down his pencil, and, rising from the table, stretched himself on a sofa at the upper end of the cabin.

'Boy,' said he, 'what is your name?'

'Ralph Rover,' I replied.

'Where did you come from, and how came you to be on that island? How many companions had you on it? Answer me, now, and mind you tell no lies.'

'I never tell lies,' said I, firmly.

I then told him the history of myself and my companions from the time we sailed till the day of his visit to the island, taking care, however, to make no mention of the Diamond Cave. After I had concluded, he was silent for a few minutes; then, looking up, he said: 'Boy, I believe you.'

I was surprised at this remark, for I could not imagine why he should not believe me.

'And what,' continued the captain, 'makes you think that this schooner is a pirate?'

'The black flag,' said I, 'showed me what you are; and if any further proof were wanting I have had it in the brutal treatment I have received at your hands.'

The captain frowned as I spoke, but subduing his anger he continued: 'Boy, you are too bold. I admit that we treated you roughly, but that was because you gave us a good deal of trouble. As to the black flag, that is merely a joke that my fellows play off upon people sometimes in order to frighten them. I am no pirate, boy, but a lawful trader – a rough one, I grant you, but one can't help that in these seas, where there are so many pirates on the water and such murderous black-guards on the land. I carry on a trade in sandalwood with the Fiji Islands; and if you choose, Ralph, to behave yourself and be a good boy, I'll take you along with me and give you a good share of the profits. You see, I'm in want of an honest boy like you, to look after the cabin and keep the log, and superintend the traffic on shore sometimes. What say you, Ralph, would you like to become a sandalwood trader?'

I was much surprised by this explanation, and a good deal relieved to find that the vessel, after all, was not a pirate; but instead of replying I said: 'If it be as you state, then why did you take me from my island, and why do you not now take me back?'

The captain smiled as he replied: 'I took you off in anger, boy, and I'm sorry for it. I would even now take you back, but we are too far away from it. See, there it is,' he added, laying his finger on the chart, 'and we are now here – fifty miles at least. It would not be fair to my men to put about now, for they have all an interest in the trade.'

I could make no reply to this; so, after a little more conversation, I agreed to become one of the crew, at least until we could reach some civilized island where I might be put ashore.

CHAPTER XI

Three weeks later I was standing on the quarterdeck of the schooner watching the gambols of a shoal of porpoises that swam round us. It was a dead calm: one of those still, hot, sweltering days, so common in the Pacific. No cloud floated in the deep blue above; no ripple broke the reflected blue below. The sun shone fiercely in the sky.

No sound broke on our ears save the soft puff now and then of a porpoise, the slow creak of the masts, as we swayed gently on the swell, and the occasional flap of the hanging sails. An awning covered the fore and after parts of the schooner, under which the men composing the watch on deck lolled in sleepy indolence, overcome with excessive heat. Bloody Bill, as the men invariably called him, was standing at the tiller, but his post for the present was a sinecure, and he whiled away the time by alternately gazing in dreamy abstraction at the compass in the binnacle, and by walking to the taffrail in order to spit into the sea. In one of these turns he came near to where I was standing, and, leaning over the side, looked long and earnestly down into the blue wave.

This man was the only human being on board with whom I had the slightest desire to become better acquainted. The other men, knowing that I was a protégé of the captain, treated me with total indifference. Bloody Bill did the same; but this was his conduct towards everyone else. As he now leaned over the taffrail close beside me, I said to him: 'Bill, why is it that you are so gloomy? Why do you never speak to anyone?'

Bill smiled slightly as he replied: 'Why, I s'pose it's because I haint got nothin' to say!'

'That's strange,' said I, musingly, 'you look like a man that could think, and such men can usually speak.'

'So they can, youngster,' rejoined Bill, somewhat sternly; 'and I could speak too if I had a mind to, but what's the use o' speakin' here? The men only open their mouths to curse and swear.'

'Well, Bill, that's true, but I don't swear, Bill, so you might talk to me sometimes, I think. I've been used to friendly conversation, Bill, and I really would take it kind if you would talk to me a little now and then.'

'An' where have you been used to friendly conversation,' said Bill, looking down again into the sea; 'not on that Coral Island, I take it?'

'Yes, indeed,' said I, energetically. 'I have spent many of the happiest months in my life on that Coral Island'; and without waiting to be further questioned, I launched out into a glowing account of the happy life that Jack and Peterkin and I had spent together, and related minutely every circumstance that befell us while on the island.

'Boy, boy,' said Bill, in a voice so deep that it startled me, 'this is no place for you.'

'That's true,' said I; 'I'm of little use on board, and I don't like my comrades; but I can't help it, and at any rate I hope to be free again soon.'

'Free?' said Bill, looking at me in surprise.

'Yes, free,' returned I; 'the captain said he would put me ashore after this trip was over.'

'*This trip!* Hark'ee, boy,' said Bill, lowering his voice, 'what said the captain to you the day you came aboard?'

'He said that he was a trader in sandalwood and no pirate, and told me that if I would join him for this trip he would give me a good share of the profits or put me on shore in some civilized island if I chose.'

Bill's brows lowered savagely as he muttered: 'Ay, he said truth when he told you he was a sandalwood trader, but he lied when –'

'Sail ho!' shouted the look-out at the mast-head.

'Where away?' cried Bill, springing to the tiller.

'On the starboard quarter, hull down, sir,' answered the look-out.

At this moment the captain came on deck, and mounting into the rigging, surveyed the sail through the glass.

'Take in top-sails!' shouted the captain, swinging himself down on the deck by the main-back stay.

'Take in top-sails!' roared the first mate.

'Ay, ay, sir-r-r!' answered the men as they sprang into the rigging and went aloft like cats.

Instantly all was bustle on board the hitherto quiet schooner. The top-sails were taken in and stowed, the men stood by the sheets and halyards, and the captain gazed anxiously at the breeze which was now rushing towards us like a sheet of dark blue. In a few seconds it struck us. The schooner trembled at the sudden onset, then bending gracefully to the wind, she cut through the waves with her sharp prow like a dolphin, while Bill directed her course towards the strange sail.

In half an hour we neared her sufficiently to make out that she was a schooner, and judged her to be a trader. She evidently did not like our appearance, for, the instant the breeze reached her, she crowded all sail and showed us her stern. As the breeze had moderated a little our top-sails were again shaken out, and it soon became evident that we doubled her speed and would overhaul her speedily. When within a mile we hoisted British colours, but receiving no acknowledgment, the captain ordered a shot to be fired across her bows. In a moment, to my surprise, a large portion of the bottom of the boat amidships was removed, and in the hole thus exposed appeared an immense brass gun. It worked on a swivel and was elevated by means of machinery. It was quickly loaded and fired. The heavy ball struck the water a few yards ahead of the chase, and, richocheting into the air, plunged into the sea a mile beyond it.

This produced the desired effect. The strange vessel hove-to, while we ranged up and lay-to, about a hundred yards off.

'Lower the boat,' cried the captain.

In a second the boat was lowered and manned by a part of the crew, all armed with cutlasses and pistols. As the captain passed me to get into it, he said: 'Jump into the stern sheets, Ralph, I may want you.' I obeyed, and in ten minutes more we were standing on the stranger's deck. We were all much surprised at the sight that met our eyes. Instead of a crew of such sailors as we were accustomed to see, there were only fifteen blacks standing on the quarterdeck and regarding us with looks of undisguised alarm. They were totally unarmed and most of them unclothed; one or two, however, wore portions of European attire. One had on a pair of duck trousers which were much too large for him. Another wore nothing but the common scanty native garment round the loins, and a black beaver hat. But the most ludicrous personage of all was a tall middle-aged man, of a mild, simple expression of countenance, who wore a white cotton shirt, a swallow-tailed coat, and a straw hat, while his black brawny legs were totally uncovered below the knees.

'Where's the commander of this ship?' enquired our captain, stepping up to this individual.

'I is capin,' he answered, taking off his straw hat and making a low bow.

'You!' said our captain, in surprise. 'Where do you come from, and where are you bound? What cargo have you aboard?'

'We is come,' answered the man with the swallow-tail, 'from Aitutaki; we was go for Rarotonga. We is native miss'-nary ship; our name is de *Olive Branch*; an' our cargo is two tons coconuts, seventy pigs, twenty cats, and de gosp'l.'

This announcement was received by the crew of our vessel with a shout of laughter, which, however, was peremptorily checked by the captain, who advanced towards the missionary and shook him warmly by the hand.

'I am very glad to have fallen in with you,' said he, 'and I wish you much success in your missionary labours. Pray take me to your cabin, as I wish to converse with you privately.'

The missionary immediately took him by the hand, and as he led him away I heard him saying: 'Me most glad to find you trader; we t'ought you be pirate. You very like one 'bout the masts.'

The captain came on deck again in a quarter of an hour, and, shaking hands cordially with the missionary, ordered us into our boat and returned to the schooner, which was immediately put before the wind. In a few minutes the *Olive Branch* was left far behind us.

That afternoon, as I was down below at dinner, I heard the men talking about this curious ship.

'I wonder,' said one, 'why our captain looked so sweet on yon swallow-tailed super-cargo o' pigs and gospels. If it had been an ordinary trader, now, he would have taken as many o' the pigs as he required and sent the ship with all on board to the bottom.'

'Why, Dick, you must be new to these seas if you don't know that,' cried another. 'The captain cares as much for the gospel as you do (an' that's precious little), but he knows, and everybody knows, that the only place among the southern islands where a ship can put in and get what she wants in comfort, is where the gospel has been sent to. There are hundreds o' islands where you might as well jump straight into a shark's maw as land without a band o' thirty comrades armed to the teeth to back you.'

'Ralph Rover!' shouted a voice down the hatchway. 'Captain wants you, aft.'

Springing up the ladder I hastened to the cabin.

On coming again on deck I found Bloody Bill at the helm, and as we were alone together I tried to draw him into conversation. After repeating to him the conversation in the forecastle about the missionaries, I said: 'Tell me, Bill, is this schooner really a trader in sandalwood?'

'Yes, Ralph, she is; but she's just as really a pirate. The black flag you saw flying at the peak was no deception.'

'Then how can you say she's a trader?' asked I.

'Why, as to that, she trades when she can't take by force,

130

but she takes by force, when she can, in preference. Ralph,' he added, lowering his voice, 'if you had seen the bloody deeds that I have witnessed done on these decks you would not need to ask if we were pirates. But you'll find it out soon enough. As for the missionaries, the captain favours them because they are useful to him.'

Our track after this lay through several clusters of small islets, among which we were becalmed more than once. During this part of our voyage the watch on deck and the look-out at the mast-head were more than usually vigilant, as we were not only in danger of being attacked by the natives, who, I learned from the captain's remarks, were a bloody and deceitful tribe at this group, but we were also exposed to much risk from the multitudes of coral reefs that rose up in the channels between the islands. Our precautions against the natives I found were indeed necessary.

One day we were becalmed among a group of small islands, most of which appeared to be uninhabited. As we were in want of fresh water the captain sent the boat ashore to bring off a cask or two. But we were mistaken in thinking there were no natives; for scarcely had we drawn near to the shore when a band of naked blacks rushed out of the bush and assembled on the beach, brandishing their clubs and spears in a threatening manner. Our men were well armed, but refrained from showing any signs of hostility, and rowed nearer in order to converse with the natives; and I now found that more than one of the crew could imperfectly speak dialects of the language peculiar to the South Sea islanders. When within forty yards of the shore, we ceased rowing, and the first mate stood up to address the multitude; but, instead of answering us, they replied with a shower of stones, some of which cut the men severely. Instantly our muskets were levelled, and a volley was about to be fired, when the captain hailed us in a loud voice from the schooner, which lay not more than five or six hundred yards off the shore.

'Don't fire!' he shouted, angrily. 'Pull off to the point ahead of you.'

The men looked surprised at this order, and uttered deep curses as they prepared to obey. Three or four of them hesitated, and seemed disposed to mutiny.

'Don't distress yourselves, lads,' said the mate, while a bitter smile curled his lip. 'Obey orders. The captain's not the man to take an insult tamely. If Long Tom does not speak presently I'll give myself to the sharks.'

The men smiled significantly as they pulled from the shore, which was now crowded with a dense mass of blacks amounting, probably, to five or six hundred. We had not rowed off above a couple of hundred yards when a loud roar thundered over the sea, and the big brass gun sent a withering shower of grape point-blank into the midst of the living mass, through which a wide lane was cut, while a yell burst from the miserable survivors as they fled to the woods. My blood curdled within me as I witnessed this frightful and wanton slaughter; but I had little time to think, for the captain's deep voice came again over the water towards us: 'Pull ashore, lads, and fill your water casks.' The men obeyed in silence, and it seemed to me as if even their hard hearts were shocked by the ruthless deed. On gaining the mouth of the rivulet at which we intended to take in water, we found it flowing with blood, for the greater part of those who were slain had been standing on the banks of the stream, a short way above its mouth. Many of the wretched creatures had fallen into it, and we found one body jammed between two rocks. No one dared to oppose our landing now, so we carried our casks to a pool above the murdered group, and having filled them, returned on board. Fortunately a breeze sprang up soon afterwards and carried us away from the dreadful spot.

'And this,' thought I, gazing in horror at the captain, who, with a quiet look of indifference leaned upon the taffrail smoking a cigar, 'this is the man who favours the missionaries because they are useful to him and can tame the savages better than anyone else can do it!'

It was many days before I recovered a little of my wonted spirits. I could not shake off the feeling that I was in a frightful dream. But I was now resolved that I would run away to the very first island we should land at. At last I made up my mind to communicate my intention to Bloody Bill; for, during several talks I had had with him of late, I felt assured that he too would willingly escape if possible. When I told him of my design he shook his head. 'No, no, Ralph,' said he, 'you must not think of running away here. Among some of the groups of islands you might do so with safety, but if you tried it here you would find that you had jumped out of the fryin'-pan into the fire.'

'How so, Bill?' said I. 'Would the natives not receive me?'

'That they would, lad, but they would eat you too.'

'Eat me!' said I in surprise. 'I thought the South Sea islanders never ate anybody except their enemies.'

'Humph!' ejaculated Bill. 'I s'pose 'twas yer tender-hearted friends in England that put that notion into your head. I know for certain that the Fiji islanders eat not only their enemies but one another; and they do it not for spite, but for pleasure. It's a *fact* that they prefer human flesh to any other. But they don't like white men's flesh so well as black. They say it makes them sick.'

'Why, Bill,' said I, 'you told me just now that they would eat *me* if they caught me.'

'So I did; and so I think they would. I've only heard some o' them say they don't like white men *so well* as black; but if they was hungry they wouldn't be particular. Anyhow, I'm sure they would kill you. You see, Ralph, I've been a good while in them parts, and I've visited the different groups of islands oftentimes as a trader. And thoroughgoin' black-guards some o' them traders are. No better than pirates, I can tell you. I'm up to the ways o' these fellows. There was a small tradin' schooner wrecked off one of these islands when we were lyin' there in harbour during a storm. The crew was lost, all but three men, who swam ashore. The moment they landed they were seized by the natives and carried up into the woods. We could not help them, for our crew was small, and if we had gone ashore they would likely have killed us all. We never saw the three men again; but we heard frightful yelling, and dancing, and merry-making that night; and one o' the natives, who came aboard to trade with us next day, told us that the *long pigs*, as he called the men, had been roasted and eaten, and their bones were to be converted into sail needles. He also said that white men were bad to eat, and that most o' the people on shore were sick.'

I was very much shocked and cast down in my mind at this horrible account of the natives, and asked Bill what he would advise me to do. Looking round the deck to make sure that we were not overheard, he lowered his voice and said: 'There are two or three ways that we might escape, Ralph, but none o' them's easy. If the captain would only sail for some o' the islands near Tahiti, we might run away there well enough, because the natives are all Christians; an' we find that wherever the savages take up with Christianity they always give over their bloody ways, and are safe to be trusted. The captain always keeps a sharp look out after us when we get to these islands, for he half suspects that one or two o' us are tired of his company.'

Bill then bade me good night, and went below, while a comrade took his place at the helm. I walked aft, and, leaning over the stern, looked down into the phosphorescent waves that gurgled around the rudder, and streamed out like a flame of blue light in the vessel's wake. My thoughts were very sad. As I thought upon Jack and Peterkin anxious forebodings crossed my mind, and I pictured to myself the grief and dismay with which they would search every nook and corner of the island, in a vain attempt to discover my dead body. I wondered, too, how Jack would succeed in getting Peterkin out of the cave without my assistance; and I trembled when I thought that he might lose presence of mind, and begin to kick when he was in the tunnel! These thoughts were suddenly interrupted and put to flight by a bright red blaze which lighted up the horizon to the southward. This appearance was accompanied by a low growling sound, as of distant thunder, and the sky above us became black, while a hot stifling wind blew in fitful gusts.

The crew assembled hastily on deck, and most of them were under the belief that a frightful hurricane was pending; but the captain, coming on deck, soon explained the phenomena.

'It's only a volcano,' said he. 'I knew there was one hereabouts, but thought it was extinct. Up there and furl top-gallant-sails; we'll likely have a breeze, and it's well to be ready.'

As he spoke, a shower began to fall, which we quickly observed was not rain, but fine ashes. As we were many miles distant from the volcano, these must have been carried to us from it by the wind. As the captain had predicted, a stiff breeze soon afterwards sprang up, under the influence of which we speedily left the volcano far behind us; but during the greater part of the night we could see its lurid glare and hear its distant thunder. The shower did not cease to fall for several hours, and we must have sailed under it for nearly forty miles, perhaps farther. When we emerged from the cloud, our decks and every part of the rigging were completely covered with a thick coat of ashes.

Three days after passing the volcano, we found ourselves a few miles to windward of an island of considerable size and luxuriant aspect. It consisted of two mountains, which seemed to be nearly four thousand feet high. They were separated from each other by a broad valley, whose thick-growing trees ascended a considerable distance up the mountain sides; and rich level plains, or meadow-land, spread round the base of the mountains. Bloody Bill was beside me when the island first hove in sight.

'Ha!' he exclaimed. 'I know that island well. They call it Emo.'

'Have you been here before, then?' I enquired

'Ay, that I have, often, and so has this schooner. 'Tis a famous island for sandalwood. We have taken many cargoes off it already, and have paid for them too; for the natives are so numerous that we dared not try to take it by force. But our captain has tried to cheat them so often, that they're beginnin' not to like us overmuch now.'

We soon ran inside the barrier coral-reef, and let go our anchor in six fathoms of water, just opposite the mouth of a small creek, whose shores were densely covered with mangroves and tall umbrageous trees. The principal village of the natives lay about half a mile from this point. Ordering the boat out, the captain jumped into it, and ordered me to follow him. The men, fifteen in number, were well armed; and the mate was directed to have Long Tom ready for emergencies.

'Give way, lads!' cried the captain.

The oars fell into the water at the word, the boat shot from the schooner's side, and in a few minutes reached the shore. Here, contrary to our expectation, we were met with the utmost cordiality by Romata, the principal chief of the island, who conducted us to his house, and gave us mats to sit upon. I observed in passing that the natives, of whom there were two or three thousand, were totally unarmed.

After a short preliminary palaver, a feast of baked pigs and various roots was spread before us; of which we partook sparingly, and then proceeded to business. The captain stated his object in visiting the island, regretted that there had been a slight misunderstanding during the last visit, and hoped that no ill-will was borne by either party.

Romata answered that he had forgotten there had been any differences between them, and assured his friends they should have every assistance in cutting and embarking the wood. The terms were afterwards agreed on, and we rose to depart. All this conversation was afterwards explained to me by Bill, who understood the language pretty well.

Romata accompanied us on board, and explained that a great chief from another island was then on a visit to him, and was to be ceremoniously entertained on the following day. After begging to be allowed to introduce him to us, and receiving permission, he sent his canoe ashore to bring him off. At the same time he gave orders to bring on board his two favourites, a cock and a parakeet. While the canoe was gone on his errand, I had time to regard the chief attentively. He was a man of immense size, with massive but beautifully moulded limbs and figure, only parts of which, the broad chest and muscular arms, were uncovered; for, although the lower orders generally wore no other clothing than a strip of cloth called *maro* round their loins, the chief, on particular occasions, wrapped his person in voluminous folds of a species of native cloth made from the bark of the Chinese paper-mulberry. Romata wore a magnificent black beard and moustache, and his hair was frizzed out to such an extent that it resembled a large turban, in which was stuck a long wooden pin! This pin served for scratching the head, for which purpose the fingers were too short. Romata, we found, slept with his head on a wooden pillow, in which was cut a hollow for the neck, so that the hair of the sleeper might not be disarranged.

In ten minutes the canoe returned, bringing the other chief, who certainly presented a most extraordinary appearance, having painted one half of his face red and the other half yellow, besides ornamenting it with various designs in black! Otherwise he was much the same in appearance as Romata, though not so powerfully built. As this chief had never seen a ship before, he was much taken up with the neatness of all the fittings of the schooner. He was particularly struck with a musket, and asked where the white men got hatchets hard enough to cut the tree of which the barrel was made! I observed that all the other natives walked in a crouching posture while in the presence of Romata. Before our guests left us, the captain ordered the brass gun to be uncovered and fired for their gratification; and I have every reason to believe he did so for the purpose of showing our superior power. Romata had never seen this gun before, and the astonishment with which he viewed it was very amusing. Being desirous of knowing its power, he begged that the captain would fire it. So a shot was put into it. The chiefs were then directed to look at a rock about two miles out at sea, and the gun was fired. In a second the top of the rock was seen to burst asunder, and to fall in fragments into the sea.

Of all the things, however, that afforded matter of amusement to these natives, that which pleased Romata's visitor most was the ship's pump. He never tired of examining it, and pumping up the water.

Next day the crew went ashore to cut sandalwood, while the captain, with one or two men, remained on board, in order to be ready, if need be, with the brass gun, which was unhoused and conspicuously elevated, with its capacious muzzle directed point-blank at the chief's house. The men were fully armed as usual; and the captain ordered me to go with them, to assist in the work.

As we wound along in single file through the rich fragrant groves of banana, coconut, bread-fruit, and other trees, I observed that there were many plum and banian trees. On turning into an open glade we came abruptly upon a cluster of native houses. They were built chiefly of bamboos, thatched with the large thick leaves of the pandanus; but many of them had little more than a sloping roof and three sides with an open front. About half a mile inland we arrived at the spot where the sandalwood grew, and, while the men set to work, I clambered up an adjoining hill to observe the country.

About midday, the chief arrived with several followers, one of whom carried a baked pig on a wooden platter, with yams and potatoes on several plantain leaves, which he presented to the men, who sat down under the shade of a tree to dine. The chief sat down to dine also; but, to my surprise, instead of feeding himself, one of his wives performed that office for him! I was seated beside Bill, and asked him the reason of this.

'It is beneath his dignity, I believe, to feed himself,' answered Bill.

'Look there,' said I, pointing to a man. 'I've seen a few of these light-skinned fellows among the Fijians. They seem to me to be of quite a different race.'

'So they are,' answered Bill. 'These fellows come from the Tongan Islands, which lie a long way to the eastward. They come here to build their big war-canoes; and as these take two, and sometimes four, years to build, there's always some o' the brown-skins among the black sarpents o' these islands.'

'By the way, Bill,' said I, 'your mentioning serpents' reminds me that I have not seen a reptile of any kind since I came to this part of the world.'

'No more there are any,' said Bill; 'there's none on the islands but a lizard or two and some such harmless things. But I never seed any myself. If there's one on the land, however, there's more than enough in the water, and that minds me of a wonderful brute they have here. But, come, I'll show it to you.' So saying, Bill arose, and, leaving the men still busy with the baked pig, led me into the forest. After a short distance we came upon a pond of stagnant water. A native lad had followed us, to whom we beckoned. On Bill saying a few words to him, the boy advanced to the edge of the pond, and gave a low peculiar whistle. Immediately the water became agitated and an enormous eel thrust its head above the surface and allowed the youth to touch it. It was about twelve feet long, and as thick round the body as a man's thigh.

'There,' said Bill, his lip curling with contempt, 'what do you think of that for a god, Ralph? This is one o' their gods, and it has been fed with dozens o' livin' babies already. How many more it'll get afore it dies is hard to say.'

'Babies?' said I, with an incredulous look.

'Ay, babies,' returned Bill. 'I tell you, Ralph, it's a *fact*. I've seed it with my own eyes. They don't feed it regularly with livin' babies, but they give it one now and then as a treat. Bah! you brute!' cried Bill, in disgust, giving the reptile a kick on the snout that sent it back into its loathsome pool. I thought it lucky for Bill, indeed for all of us, that the native youth's back happened to be turned at the time! As we retraced our steps I questioned my companion further on this subject.

'How comes it, Bill, that the mothers allow such a dreadful thing to be done?'

'Allow it? The mothers *do* it! One o' their customs is to murder their infants the moment they are born, burying them alive and stamping them to death while under the sod.'

I felt sick at heart while my companion recited these horrors.

'But it's a curious fact,' he continued, after a pause, 'it's a curious fact, that wherever the missionaries get a footin' all these things come to an end at once, an' the savages take to doin' each other good, and singin' psalms, just like Methodists.'

CHAPTER XII

Next day the wood-cutting party went ashore again, and I accompanied them as before. During the dinner hour I wandered into the woods alone, being disinclined for food that day. I had not rambled far when I found myself unexpectedly on the seashore. Here I found a party of the islanders busy with one of their war-canoes, which was almost ready for launching. I stood for a long time watching this party with great interest, and observed that they fastened the timbers and planks to each other very much as I had seen Jack fasten those of our little boat. But what surprised me most was its immense length, which I found to be a hundred feet; and it was so capacious that it could have held three hundred men. It had the unwieldy out-rigger and enormously high stern-posts which I had remarked on the canoe that came to us while I was on the Coral Island. Observing some boys playing at games a short way along the beach, I resolved to go and watch them.

Advancing towards the children, I sat down on a grassy bank under the shade of a plantain tree, to watch them. And a happier or more noisy crew I have never seen. There were at least two hundred of them, both boys and girls, all of whom were clad in no other garments than their own glossy little black skins, except the *maro*, or strip of cloth round the loins of the boys, and a very short petticoat or kilt on the girls. They did not all play at the same game, but amused themselves in different groups.

One band was busily engaged in a game exactly similar to our blind-man's-buff. Another set were walking on stilts, which raised the children three feet from the ground. They were very expert at this amusement and seldom tumbled. In another place were a number of boys engaged in flying kites. But the kites were different from ours in many respects, being of every variety of shape. They were made of very thin cloth, and the boys raised them to a wonderful height in the air by means of twine from the coconut husk. But the amusement which the greatest number of the children of both sexes seemed to take chief delight in was swimming and diving in the sea; and the expertness which they exhibited was truly amazing. They never seemed to tire of this sport, and, from the great heat of the water in the South Seas, they could remain in it nearly all day without feeling chilled. Many of these children were almost infants, scarce able to walk.

I suppose it was in honour of their guest that a grand swimming match was got up, for Romata came and told the captain that they were going to engage in surf-swimming, and begged him to 'come and see'.

'What sort of amusement is this surf-swimming?' I enquired of Bill, as we walked together to a part of the shore on which several thousands of the natives were assembled.

'It's a very favourite lark with these 'xtr'or'nary critters,' replied Bill. 'Ye see, I s'pose they found swimmin' for miles out to sea, and divin' fathoms deep, wasn't exciting enough, so they invented this game o' swimmin' on the surf. Each man and boy has got a short board or plank, with which he swims out for a mile or more to sea, and then, gettin' on the top o' yon thunderin' breaker, they come to shore on the top of it, yellin' and screechin' like fiends. It's a marvel to me that they're not dashed to shivers on the coral reef. But there they go!'

As he spoke, several hundreds of the natives uttered a loud yell, rushed down the beach, plunged into the surf, and were carried off by the seething foam of the retreating wave.

At the point where we stood, the encircling coral reef joined the shore, so that the magnificent breakers fell in thunder at the feet of the multitudes who lined the beach. For some time the swimmers continued to strike out to sea, breasting over the swell like hundreds of black seals. Then they all turned, and, watching an approaching billow, mounted its white crest, and, each laying his breast on the short flat board, came rolling towards the shore, careering on the summit of the mighty wave. Just as the monster wave curled in solemn majesty to fling its bulky length upon the beach, most of the swimmers slid back into the trough behind; others, slipping off their boards, seized them in their hands, and, plunging through the watery waste, swam out to repeat the amusement; but a few, who seemed to me the most reckless, continued their career until they were launched upon the beach, and enveloped in the churning foam and spray. One of these last came in on the crest of the wave most manfully, and landed with a violent bound almost on the spot where Bill and I stood. I saw by his peculiar head-dress that he was the chief whom the tribe entertained as their guest. The sea-water had removed nearly all the paint with which his face had been covered; and, as he rose panting to his feet, I recognized, to my surprise, the features of Tararo, my old friend of the Coral Island!

Tararo at the same moment recognized me, and, advancing quickly, took me round the neck and rubbed noses; which had the effect of transferring a good deal of the moist paint from his nose to mine. Then, recollecting that this was not the white man's mode of salutation, he grasped me by the hand and shook it violently.

'Hallo, Ralph!' cried Bill, in surprise, 'that chap seems to be an old acquaintance.'

'Right, Bill,' I replied, 'he is indeed an old acquaintance': and I explained in a few words that he was the chief whose party Jack and Peterkin and I had helped to save.

Tararo entered into an animated conversation with Bill, pointing frequently during the course of it to me; whereby I concluded he must be telling him about the memorable battle, and the part we had taken in it. When he paused, I begged of Bill to ask him about the woman Avatea, for I had some hope that she might have come with Tararo on this visit. 'And ask him,' said I, 'who she is, for I am persuaded she is of a different race from the Feejeeans.' On the mention of her name the chief frowned darkly, and seemed to speak with much anger.

'You're right, Ralph,' said Bill, when the chief had ceased to talk; 'she's not a Feejee girl, but a Samoan. The chief says she was taken in war, and that he got her three years ago, an' kept her as his daughter ever since. Lucky for her, poor girl, else she'd have been roasted and eaten like the rest.'

'But why does Tararo frown and look so angry?' said I.

'Because the girl's obstinate, an' won't marry the man he wants her to. It seems that a chief of some other land came on a visit to Tararo and took a fancy to her, but she wouldn't have him on no account, bein' already in love with a young chief whom Tararo hates, and she kicked up a desperate shindy; so, as he was going on a war expedition in his canoe, he left her to think about it, sayin' he'd be back in six months or so, when he hoped she wouldn't be so obstropolous. This happened just a week ago; an' Tararo says that if she's not ready to go, when the chief returns, as his bride, she'll be sent to him as a *long pig*.'

'As a long pig!' I exclaimed in surprise. 'Why, what does he mean by that?'

'He means somethin' very unpleasant,' answered Bill, with a frown. 'You see, these blackguards eat men an' women just as readily as they eat pigs; and, as baked pigs and baked men are very like each other in appearance, they call men *long* pigs. If Avatea goes to this fellow as a long pig, it's all up with her, poor thing.'

'Is she on the island now?' I asked, eagerly.

'No, she's at Tararo's island.'

'And where does it lie?'

'About fifty or sixty miles to the south'ard o' this,' returned Bill; 'but I —'

At this moment we were startled by the cry of 'Mao! mao! — a shark! a shark!' which was immediately followed by a shriek. We turned hastily and had just time to observe the glaring eyeballs of one of the swimmers as he tossed his arms in the air. Next instant he was pulled under the waves. A canoe was instantly launched, and the hand of the drowning man was caught, but only half of his body was dragged from the maw of the monster.

In most countries of the world this would have made a deep impression on the spectators, but the only effect it had upon these islanders was to make them hurry with all speed out of the sea.

After this the natives had a series of wrestling and boxing matches; and being men of immense size and muscle, they did a good deal of injury to each other, especially in boxing.

Next day, while we were returning from the woods to our schooner, we observed Romata rushing about in the neighbourhood of his house, apparently mad with passion.

'Ah!' said Bill to me. 'There he's at his old tricks again. That's his way when he gets drink. The natives make a sort of drink o' their own, and it makes him bad enough; but when he gets brandy he's like a wild tiger. The captain, I suppose, has given him a bottle, as usual, to keep him in good humour. After drinkin' he usually goes to sleep, and the people keep out of his way, for fear they should waken him. When he's waked up, he rushes out just as you see him now, and spears or clubs the first person he meets.'

It seemed at the present time, however, that no deadly weapon had been in his way, for the infuriated chief was raging about without one. Suddenly he caught sight of an unfortunate man who was trying to conceal himself behind a tree. Rushing towards him, Romata struck him a terrible blow on the head, which knocked out the poor man's eye and also dislocated the chief's finger.

'Have these wretched creatures no law among themselves,' said I, 'which can restrain such wickedness?'

'None,' replied Bill. 'The chief's word is law. He might kill and eat a dozen of his own subjects any day for nothing more than his own pleasure, and nobody would take the least notice of it.'

Next morning I awoke with a feverish brow and a feeling of deep depression. I was surrounded on all sides by human beings of the most dreadful character, to whom the shedding of blood was mere pastime. On shore were the natives, whose practices were so horrible that I could not think of them without shuddering. On board were none but pirates of the blackest dye, who, although not cannibals, were foul murderers, and more blameworthy even than the savages, inasmuch as they knew better. Even Bill was so fierce in his nature as to have acquired the title of 'Bloody' from his vile companions.

When the captain came on deck, before the hour at which the men usually started for the woods, I begged of him to permit me to remain aboard that day, as I did not feel well; but he looked at me angrily, and ordered me, in a surly tone, to get ready to go on shore as usual. The fact was that the captain had been out of humour for some time past. Romata and he had had some differences, and high words had passed between them. A bad feeling had been raised and old sores had been opened.

I had, therefore, to go with the wood-cutters that day. Before starting, however, the captain called me into his cabin, and said: 'Here, Ralph, I've got a mission for you, lad. That blackguard Romata is in the dumps, and nothing will mollify him but a gift; so do you go up to his house and give him these whales' teeth, with my compliments. Take with you one of the men who can speak the language.'

I looked at the gift in some surprise, for it consisted of six white whales' teeth, and two of the same dyed bright red, which seemed to me very paltry things. Gathering them up, I left the cabin and was soon on my way to the chief's house, accompanied by Bill. On expressing my surprise at the gift, he said: 'They're paltry enough to you or me, Ralph, but they're considered of great value by them chaps. They're a sort o' cash among them. The red ones are the most prized, one of them bein' equal to twenty o' the white ones.'

On arriving at the house we found Romata sitting on a

mat. He received us rather haughtily, but on Bill explaining the nature of our errand he became very condescending, and his eyes glistened with satisfaction when he received the whales' teeth.

'Go,' said he, with a wave of the hand, 'go, tell your captain that he may cut wood today, but not tomorrow. He must come ashore – I want to have a palaver with him.'

As we left the house to return to the woods, Bill shook his head.

'There's mischief brewin' in that black rascal's head. I know him of old. But what comes here?'

As he spoke, we heard the sound of laughter and shouting in the wood, and presently there issued from it a band of natives, in the midst of whom were a number of men bearing burdens on their shoulders. At first I thought that these burdens were poles with something rolled round them, the end of each pole resting on a man's shoulder. But on a nearer approach I saw that they were human beings, tied hand and foot, and lashed to the poles. I counted twenty of them as they passed.

'More murder!' said Bill, in a voice that sounded between a hoarse laugh and a groan.

'Surely they are not going to murder them?' said I.

As we continued our way towards the woodcutters, Bill looked anxiously over his shoulder, in the direction where the procession had disappeared. At last he stopped, and turning abruptly on his heel, said: 'I must be at the bottom o' that affair, Ralph. Let us follow these black scoundrels and see what they're goin' to do.'

We passed rapidly through the bush, being guided by the shouts of the savages. Suddenly there was a dead silence, which continued for some time, while Bill and I involuntarily quickened our pace until we were running at the top of our speed. As we reached the verge of the wood, we discovered the savages surrounding the large war-canoe, which they were apparently on the point of launching. Suddenly the multitude put their united strength to the canoe; but scarcely had the huge machine begun to move, when a yell rose high above the shouting of the savages. It had not died away when another and another smote upon my throbbing ear; and then I saw that these inhuman monsters were actually launching their canoe over the living bodies of their victims. Forward they went in ruthless indifference, shouting as they went, while high above their voices rang the dying shrieks of those wretched creatures, as, one after another, the ponderous canoe passed over them, burst the eyeballs from their sockets, and sent the life's blood gushing from their mouths.

When it was over I turned round and fell upon the grass with a deep groan; but Bill seized me by the arm, and cried: 'Come along, lad; let's away!' And so, staggering and stumbling over the tangled underwood, we fled from the fatal spot.

During the remainder of that day I felt as if I were in a horrible dream. I scarce knew what was said to me. At last the hour to return aboard came. We marched down to the beach, and I felt relief for the first time when my feet rested on the schooner's deck.

In the course of the evening I overheard part of a conversation between the captain and the first mate, which startled me not a little. They were down in the cabin, and conversed in an undertone, but the skylight being off, I overheard every word that was said.

'I don't half like it,' said the mate. 'It seems to me that we'll only have hard fightin' and no pay.'

'No pay!' repeated the captain, in a voice of suppressed anger. 'Do you call a good cargo all for nothing no pay?'

'Very true,' returned the mate; 'but we've got the cargo aboard. Why not cut your cable and take French leave o' them? What's the use o' tryin' to lick the blackguards when it'll do us no manner o' good?'

'Mate,' said the captain, in a low voice, 'you talk like a fresh-water sailor. Surely' – his voice assumed a slightly sneering tone as he said this – 'surely I am not to suppose that *you* have become soft-hearted! Besides, you are wrong in regard to the cargo being aboard; there's a good quarter of it lying in the woods, and that blackguard chief knows it and won't let me take it off. He defied us to do our worst, yesterday. I intend to muffle the sweeps and row the schooner up to the head of the creek there, from which point we can command the pile of sandalwood with our gun. Then I shall land with all the men except two, who will be ready with the boat to take us off. We can creep through the woods to the head of the village, where these cannibals are always dancing round their suppers of human flesh, and if the carbines of the men are loaded with a heavy charge of buck-shot, we can drop forty or fifty at the first volley. After that the thing will be easy enough. The savages will take to the mountains in a body, and we shall take what we require, up anchor, and away.'

To this plan the mate at length agreed. As he left the cabin I heard the captain say: 'Give the men an extra glass of grog, and don't forget the buck-shot.'

I heard this murderous conversation with horror. I immediately repeated it to Bill, who seemed much perplexed about it. At length he said: 'I'll tell you what I'll do, Ralph: I'll swim ashore after dark and fix a musket to a tree not far from the place where we'll have to land, and I'll tie a long string to the trigger, so that when our fellows cross it they'll let it off, and so alarm the village in time to prevent an attack, but not in time to prevent us gettin' back to the boat; so, master captain,' added Bill, 'you'll be baulked at least for once in your life by Bloody Bill.'

After it grew dark, Bill put his resolve in practice. He slipped over the side with a musket, swam ashore and entered the woods. He soon returned, having accomplished his purpose.

When the hour of midnight approached, the men were mustered on deck, the cable was cut and the muffled sweeps got out. These sweeps were immensely large oars, each requiring a couple of men to work it. In a few minutes we entered the mouth of the creek. Having reached the spot where we intended to land, a small kedge anchor attached to a thin line was let softly down over the stern.

'Now, lads,' whispered the captain, 'don't be in a hurry; aim low, and don't waste your first shots.'

He then pointed to the boat, into which the men crowded in silence. There was no room to row, but oars were not needed, as a slight push against the side of the schooner sent the boat gliding to the shore.

'There's no need of leaving two in the boat,' whispered the mate, as the men stepped out. 'Let Ralph stay.'

The captain assented, and ordered me to stand in readiness with the boat-hook, to shove ashore at a moment's notice if they should return, or to shove off if any of the natives should happen to approach. He glided through the bushes followed by his men. With a throbbing heart I awaited the result of our plan. I knew the exact locality where the musket was placed, for Bill had described it to me. But no sound came, and I began to fear that either they had gone in another direction or that Bill had not fixed the string properly. Suddenly I heard a faint click, and observed one or two bright sparks among the bushes. My heart sank within me, for I knew at once that the trigger had indeed been pulled but that the priming had not caught. The plan had utterly failed. A feeling of dread now began to creep over me as I stood in the boat, in that dark, silent spot, awaiting the issue of this murderous expedition. Her tapering masts were lost among the trees which overshadowed her.

Suddenly I heard a shot. In a moment a thousand voices raised a yell in the village; again the cry rose on the night air, followed by broken shouts as of scattered parties of men bounding into the woods. Then I heard another shout loud and close at hand. It was the voice of the captain cursing the man who had fired the premature shot. Then came the order, 'Forward,' followed by the wild hurrah of our men, as they charged the natives. Shots now rang in quick succession, and at last a loud volley startled the echoes of the woods. It was followed by a multitude of wild shrieks, which were immediately drowned in another 'hurrah' from the men; they were driving their enemies before them towards the sea.

While I was listening intently to these sounds, I was startled by the rustling of the leaves not far from me. At first I thought it was a party of natives who had observed the schooner, but I was speedily undeceived by observing a body of them bounding through the woods towards the scene of the battle. I saw at once that this was a party who had outflanked our men, and would speedily attack them in the rear. And so it turned out, for the shouts increased tenfold, and among them I thought I heard a death-cry uttered by voices familiar to my ear.

At length the tumult of battle ceased, and, from the cries of exultation that now arose from the natives, I felt assured that our men had been conquered. I was immediately thrown into dreadful consternation. What was I now to do? To take the schooner out of the creek without assistance was impossible. I resolved, however, to make the attempt, as being my only hope. I seized the boat-hook to push from the shore when a man sprang from the bushes.

'Stop! Ralph, stop! – There now, push off,' he cried, and bounded into the boat so violently as nearly to upset her. It was Bill's voice! In another moment we were on board – the boat made fast, the line of the anchor cut, and the sweeps run out. The schooner now began to glide quickly down the creek, but before we reached its mouth, a yell from a thousand voices on the bank told that we were discovered. Instantly a number of the natives plunged into the water and swam towards us; but we were making so much way that they could not overtake us. One, however, an immensely powerful man, succeeded in laying hold of the cut rope that hung from the stern, and clambered quickly upon deck. Bill caught sight of him the instant his head appeared above the taffrail. But he did not cease to row, and did not appear even to notice the savage until he was within a yard of him; then, dropping the sweep, he struck him a blow on the forehead with his clenched fist that felled him to the deck. Lifting him up he hurled him overboard and resumed the oar. But now a greater danger awaited us, for the natives had outrun us on the bank and were about to plunge into the water ahead of the schooner. For one moment Bill stood irresolute. Then, drawing a pistol from his belt, he sprang to the brass gun, held the pan of his pistol over the touch-hole and fired. The shot was succeeded by the hiss of the cannon's priming, then the blaze and the crashing thunder of the monstrous gun burst upon the natives with a deafening roar.

This was enough. The moment of surprise caused by the unwonted sound gave us time to pass the point; a gentle breeze bulged out our sails; the schooner bent before it, and the shouts of the disappointed natives grew fainter and fainter in the distance as we were slowly wafted out to sea.

CHAPTER XIII

When the expedition was planned, my anxieties and energies had been so powerfully aroused that I went through that terrible night without slightest fatigue. No sooner was the last fear of danger past, however, than my faculties were utterly relaxed; and, when I heard the waves rippling at the schooner's prow, as we left the hated island behind us, my senses forsook me and I fell in a swoon upon the deck.

From this state I was quickly aroused by Bill, who shook me by the arm, saying: 'Ralph, boy, rouse up, lad, we're safe now. Poor thing, I believe he's fainted. Here, take a drop o' this, it'll do you good, my boy,' he added, while he held a brandy-flask to my lips.

I raised my eyes gratefully, as I swallowed a mouthful; next moment my head sank heavily upon my arm and I fell fast asleep. I slept long, for when I awoke the sun was a good way above the horizon. I did not move on first opening my eyes. The sea seemed a sheet of undulating crystal, tipped and streaked with the saffron hues of sunrise. My mind was recalled suddenly and painfully to the present by the sight of Bill, who was seated on the deck at my feet with his head reclining, as if in sleep, on his right arm, which rested on the tiller. The slight noise I made in raising myself on my elbow caused him to start and look around.

On beholding his countenance I sprang up in anxiety. He was deadly pale, and his hair, which hung in dishevelled locks over his face, was clotted with blood. Blood also stained his hollow cheeks and covered the front of his shirt.

'Oh, Bill!' said I, with deep anxiety, 'what is the matter with you? You must have been wounded.'

'Even so, lad,' said Bill, in a soft voice, 'I've got an ugly wound, I fear, and I've been waiting for you to waken, to ask you to get me a drop o' brandy and a mouthful o' bread from the cabin lockers. I don't feel up to much just now.'

I ran below immediately, and returned with a bottle of brandy and some broken biscuit. He seemed much refreshed after eating a few morsels and drinking a long draught of water mingled with a little of the spirits. Immediately afterwards he fell asleep, and I watched him anxiously until he awoke.

'Ha!' he exclaimed, after a slumber of an hour. 'I'm the better of that nap, Ralph; I feel twice the man I was'; and he attempted to rise, but sank back again immediately with a deep groan.

'Nay, Bill, you must not move, but lie still while I look at your wound. I'll make a comfortable bed for you here on deck, and get you some breakfast. After that you shall tell me how you got it. Cheer up, Bill,' I added, seeing that he turned his head away; 'you'll be all right in a little, and I'll be a capital nurse to you though I'm no doctor.'

I then left him, and lighted a fire in the caboose. While it was kindling, I went to the steward's pantry and procured the materials for a good breakfast.

'Now then, Bill,' said I, cheerfully, 'let's fall to. I'm very hungry myself, I can tell you; but – I forgot – your wound,' I added, rising; 'let me look at it.'

I found that the wound was caused by a pistol shot in the chest. It did not bleed much, and, as it was on the right side, I was in hopes that it might not be very serious. But Bill shook his head. 'However,' said he, 'sit down, Ralph, and I'll tell you all about it.

'You see, after we left the boat an' began to push through the bushes, we went straight for the line of my musket, as I had expected; but by some unlucky chance it didn't explode; I fancy the priming had got damp and didn't catch. I was in a great quandary now what to do, for I couldn't concoct any good reason for firin' off my piece. Just as I was givin' it up a sudden thought came into my head. I stepped out before the rest, seemin' to be awful anxious to be at the natives, tripped my foot on a fallen tree, plunged head foremost into a bush, an' ov coorse, my carbine exploded! Then came such a screechin' from the camp as I never heard in all my life. I rose at once, and was rushin' on with the rest when the captain called a halt.

'"You did that a-purpose, you villain!" he said, with a tremendous oath, and, drawin' a pistol from his belt, let fly right into my breast. I fell at once, and remembered no more till I was brought round by the most awful yell I ever heard in my life. Jumpin' up, I looked round, and saw a fire gleamin' not far off, the light o' which showed me the captain and men tied hand and foot, each to a post, and the savages dancin' round them like demons. I saw one o' them go up to the captain flourishing a knife. He plunged it into his breast, while another yell rang upon my ear. I didn't wait for more, but, bounding up, went crashing through the bushes into the woods. The black fellows caught sight of me, however, but not in time to prevent me jumpin' into the boat.'

Bill seemed to be much exhausted after this recital.

'But now, Bill,' said I, 'it behoves us to think what course of action we shall pursue. Here we are, on the wide Pacific, in a well-appointed schooner, and the world lies before us. Moreover, here comes a breeze, so we must make up our minds which way to steer.'

'Ralph, boy,' said my companion, 'it matters not to me which way we go. I fear that my time is short now. Go where you will. I'm content.'

'Well, then, Bill, I think we had better steer to the Coral Island, and see what has become of my deer old comrades, Jack and Peterkin. I believe the island has no name, but the captain once pointed it out to me on the chart, and I marked it afterwards; so, as we know pretty well our position just now, I think I can steer to it. Then, as to working the vessel, it is true I cannot hoist the sails single-handed, but luckily we have enough of sail set already, and if it should come on to blow a squall, I could at least drop the peaks of the main and foresails, and clew them up partially without help. And if we have continued light breezes, I'll rig up a complication of blocks and fix them to the topsail halyards, so that I shall be able to hoist the sails without help. 'Tis true I'll require half a day to hoist them, but we don't need to mind that. Then I'll make a sort of erection on deck to screen you from the sun, Bill; and if you can only manage to sit beside the tiller and steer for two hours every day, so as to let me get a nap, I'll engage to let you off duty all the rest of the twenty-four hours. And if you don't feel able for steering, I'll lash the helm and heave to, while I get you your breakfasts and dinners; and so we'll manage famously and soon reach Coral Island.'

Bill smiled faintly as I ran on in this strain.

'And what will you do,' said he, 'if it comes on to blow a storm?'

This question silenced me, while I considered what I should do in such a case. At length I laid my hand on his arm, and said: 'Bill, when a man has done all that he *can* do, he ought to leave the rest to God.'

'Oh, Ralph,' said my companion, in a faint voice, looking anxiously into my face, 'I wish that I had the feelin's about God that you seem to have, at this hour. I'm dyin', Ralph; yet I, who have braved death a hundred times, am afraid to die. I'm afraid to enter the next reckoning when I go there.'

He sank back with a deep groan. As if the very elements sympathized with this man's sufferings, a low moan came sweeping over the sea.

'Hist! Ralph,' said Bill, opening his eyes; 'there's a squall coming, lad. Look alive, boy. Clew up the foresail. Drop the mainsail peak. Them squalls come quick sometimes.'

I had already started to my feet, and saw that a heavy squall was indeed bearing down on us. I instantly did as Bill desired, for the schooner was still lying motionless on the glassy sea. Having done my best to shorten sail, I returned aft, and took my stand at the helm.

'Now, boy,' said Bill, in a faint voice, 'keep her close to the wind.'

The wind burst upon us, and the spray dashed over our decks. For a time the schooner stood it bravely, and sprang forward against the rising sea like a war-horse. The sea began to rise in huge billows. There was still too much sail on the schooner, and I feared that the masts would be torn out of her or carried away, while the wind whistled and shrieked through the strained rigging. Suddenly the wind shifted a point, a heavy sea struck us on the bow, and the schooner was almost laid on her beam-ends, so that I could scarcely keep my legs. At the same moment Bill lost his hold of the belaying-pin which had served to steady him, and slid with stunning violence against the skylight. As he lay on the deck close beside me, I could see that the shock had rendered him insensible, but I did not dare to quit the tiller for an instant. At the end of that time the squall passed away, and left us rocking on the bosom of the agitated sea.

My first care, the instant I could quit the helm, was to raise Bill from the deck and place him on the couch. I then ran below for the brandy bottle and rubbed his face and hands with it, and endeavoured to pour a little down his throat. But my efforts, although I continued them long and assiduously, were of no avail – the pirate was dead!

It was with feelings of awe, not unmingled with fear, that I now seated myself on the cabin skylight and gazed upon the rigid features of my late comrade. Then I tied a cannon ball to his feet and, with feelings of the deepest sorrow, consigned him to the deep.

For fully a week after that a steady breeze blew from the east, and I made rapid progress towards my destination. From the day of setting sail from the island of the savages, I had kept a dead reckoning, and I hoped to hit the Coral Island without much difficulty.

As the weather seemed now quite settled and fine, and as I had got into the trade-winds, I set about preparations for hoisting the topsails. This was a most arduous task, and my first attempts were complete failures, owing, in a great degree, to my ignorance of mechanical forces. In my next attempt I unreeved the tackling and fitted up larger blocks and ropes. But the machinery was now so massive and heavy that the mere friction and stiffness of the thick cordage prevented me from moving it at all. Afterwards, however, I came to proportion things more correctly.

After the tackling was in good working order, it took me the greater part of a day to hoist the main-top sail. As I could not steer and work at this at the same time, I lashed the helm in such a position that it kept the schooner in her proper course. By this means I was able to go about the deck and down below for things that I wanted, as occasion required; also to cook and eat my victuals. But I did not dare to trust this plan during the three hours of rest that I allowed myself at night, as the wind might have shifted, in which case I should have been blown far out of my course. I was, there-fore, in the habit of *heaving-to* during those three hours; that is, fixing the rudder and the sails in such a position as that by acting against each other, they would keep the ship station-ary.

Of course I was to some extent anxious lest another squall should come, but I made the best provision I could in the circumstances. I proposed to keep a sharp look-out on the barometer in the cabin, and if I observed at any time a sudden fall in it, I would instantly set about my multiform appliances for reducing sail, so as to avoid being taken unawares. Thus I sailed prosperously for two weeks, with a fair wind, so that I calculated I must be drawing near to the Coral Island; at the thought of which my heart bounded with joyful expectation.

On the evening of my fourteenth day, I was awakened out of a nap by a loud cry, and starting up, I gazed around me. I was surprised and delighted to see a large albatross soaring majestically over the ship. I immediately took it into my head that this was the albatross I had seen at Penguin Island. I had, of course, no good reason for supposing this, but the idea occurred to me and I cherished it, and regarded the bird with as much affection as if he had been an old friend. He kept me company all that day and left me as night fell.

Next morning as I stood motionless and with heavy eyes at the helm, for I had not slept well, I began to weary anxiously for daylight, and peered towards the horizon, where I thought I observed something like a black cloud against the dark sky. Being always on the alert for squalls, I ran to the bow. There could be no doubt it was a squall, and as I listened I thought I heard the murmur of the coming gale. Instantly I began to work might and main at my cumbrous tackle for shortening sail, and in the course of an hour and a half had the most of it reduced. While thus engaged the dawn advanced, and I cast an occasional furtive glance ahead in the midst of my labour. But now that things were prepared for the worst, I ran forward again and looked anxiously over the bow. I now heard the roar of the waves distinctly, and as a single ray of the rising sun gleamed over the ocean I saw – what! could it be that I was dreaming? – that magnificent breaker with its ceaseless roar – yes, once more I beheld the Coral Island!

I almost fell upon the deck with the tumult of mingled emotions that filled my heart, as I gazed ardently towards my beautiful island. It was still many miles away, but sufficiently near to enable me to trace distinctly the well-remembered outlines of the two mountains. Then I went below for the telescope, and spent nearly ten minutes of the utmost impatience in vainly trying to get a focus, and in rubbing the skin nearly off my eyes, before I discovered that having previously taken off the large glass to examine something I had omitted to put it on again.

The remainder of the time I spent in making feverish preparations for arriving and seeing my dear comrades. I remembered that they were not in the habit of rising before six, and, as it was now only three, I hoped to arrive before they were awake. I set about making ready to let go the anchor, resolving in my own mind that, as I knew the depth of water in the passage of the reef and within the lagoon, I would run the schooner in and bring up opposite the bower. Fortunately the anchor was hanging at the cathead, otherwise I should never have been able to use it. Now, I had only to cut the tackling, and it would drop of its own weight. After searching among the flags, I found the terrible black one, which I ran up to the peak. While I was doing this, a thought struck me. I went to the powder magazine, brought up a blank cartridge and loaded the big brass gun, which was unhoused when we set sail. I took care to grease its mouth well, and, before leaving the fore part of the ship, thrust the poker into the fire.

All was now ready. A steady five-knot breeze was blowing, so that I was now not more than quarter of a mile from the reef. I was soon at the entrance, and the schooner glided quickly through. On coming opposite the Water Garden, I put the helm hard down. The schooner came round with a rapid, graceful bend, and lost way just opposite the bower. Running forward, I let go the anchor, caught up the red-hot poker, applied it to the brass gun, and saluted the mountains with a *bang*.

Effective although it was, however, it was scarcely equal to the bang with which, instantly after, Peterkin bounded from the bower, in scanty costume, his eyeballs starting from his head with surprise and terror. One gaze he gave, one yell, and then fled into the bushes like a wild cat. The next moment Jack went through exactly the same performance.

'Hallo!' I shouted, almost mad with joy. 'What-ho! Peterkin! Jack! hallo! it's *me*!'

My shout was just in time to arrest them. They halted and turned around, and I saw that they recognized my voice, by both of them running at full speed towards the beach. I could no longer contain myself. Throwing off my jacket, I jumped overboard at the same moment that Jack bounded into the sea. In another moment we met in deep water, clasped each other round the neck, and sank, as a matter of course, to the bottom! We were wellnigh choked, and instantly struggled to the surface, where Peterkin was spluttering about like a wounded duck, and choking himself with salt water!

During the greater part of the next three days Peterkin did nothing but roast pigs, taro, and bread-fruit, and ply me with plantains, plums, potatoes, and coconuts, while I related to him and Jack the terrible and wonderful adventures I had gone through. After I had finished the account, they made me go all over it again. They were much affected by what I told them of the probable fate of Avatea, and Peterkin could by no means brook the idea of the poor girl being converted into a *long pig*! As for Jack, he clenched his teeth, and shook his fist towards the sea, saying at the same time, that he was sorry he had not broken Tararo's head. After they had 'pumped me dry,' as Peterkin said, I begged to be informed of what had happened to them during my long absence, and particularly as to how they got out of the Diamond Cave.

'Well,' began Jack, 'after you had dived out of the cave, we waited very patiently for half an hour, not expecting you to return before the end of that time. Then we began to upbraid you for staying so long, when you knew we would be anxious; but when an hour passed, we became alarmed, and I resolved at all hazards to dive out, and see what had become of you, although I felt for poor Peterkin, because, as he truly said, "If you never come back, I'm shut up here for life." However, I promised not to run any risk, and he let me go; which, to say truth, I thought very courageous of him!'

'I should just think it was!' interrupted Peterkin.

'Well,' continued Jack, 'you may guess my consternation when you did not answer to my halloo. At first I imagined that the pirates must have killed you, and left you in the bush, or thrown you into the sea; then it occurred to me that this would have served no end of theirs, so I came to the conclusion that they must have carried you away with them. As this thought struck me, I observed the pirate schooner standing away to the nor'ard, almost hull down on the horizon, and I sat down on the rocks to watch her as she slowly sank from my sight. And I tell you, Ralph, my boy, that I shed more tears that time, at losing you, than I have done, I verily believe, all my life before. Well, after the schooner had disappeared, I dived back into the cave, much to Peterkin's relief, and told him what I had seen. We agreed to make a regular, systematic search through the woods, so as to make sure that you had not been killed. But now we thought of the difficulty of getting out of the cave without your help. Peterkin became dreadfully nervous when he thought of this; and I must confess that I felt some alarm, for, of course, I could not hope alone to take him out so quickly as we two together had brought him in. However, there was no help for it, and I endeavoured to calm his fears as well as I could: "for," said I, "you can't live here, Peterkin"; to which he replied: "Of course not, Jack, I can only die here, and, as that's not at all desirable, you had better propose something." So I suggested that he should take a good long breath, and trust himself to me.

'"Might we not make a large bag of coconut cloth, into which I cold shove my head, and tie it tight round my neck?" he asked, with a haggard smile. "It might let me get one breath under water!"

'"No use," said I; "it would fill in a moment and suffocate you. I see nothing for it, Peterkin, if you really can't keep your breath so long, but to let me knock you down, and carry you out while in a state of insensibility."

'But Peterkin didn't relish this idea. At last I got him persuaded to try to hold his breath, and commit himself to me; so down we went. But I had not got him half-way through, when he began to struggle and kick like a wild bull, burst from my grasp, and hit against the roof of the tunnel. I was, therefore, obliged to force him violently back into the cave again, where he rose panting to the surface. The upshot of it was, that we had to hold another consultation on the point, and I really believe that, had it not been for a happy thought of mine, we should have been consulting there yet.'

'I wish we had,' again interrupted Peterkin with a sigh. 'I'm sure, Ralph, if I had thought that you were coming back again, I would willingly have awaited your return for months, rather than have endured the mental agony which I went through! But proceed.'

'The thought was this,' continued Jack, 'that I should tie Peterkin's hands and feet with cords, and then lash him firmly to a stout pole about five feet long, in order to render him quite powerless, and keep him straight and stiff. You should have seen his face of horror, Ralph, when I suggested this: but he came to see that it was his only chance, and told me to set about it as fast as I could. I soon procured the cordage and a suitable pole, with which I returned to the cave, and lashed him as stiff and straight as an Egyptian mummy.

'"Now," said Peterkin, in a tremulous voice, "swim with me as near to the edge of the hole as you can before you dive, then let me take a long breath, and, as I shan't be able to speak after I've taken it, watch my face, and the moment you see me wink – dive! And oh!" he added, earnestly, "pray don't be long!"

'I promised to pay the strictest attention to his wishes, and swam with him to the outlet of the cave. "Now then," said I, "pull away at the wind, lad."

'Peterkin drew in a breath so long that I could not help thinking of the frog in the fable, that wanted to swell itself as big as the ox. Then I looked into his face earnestly. Slap went the lid of his right eye; down went my head, and up went my heels. We shot through the passage like an arrow, and rose to the surface of the open sea before you could count twenty!

'Peterkin had taken in such an awful load of wind that, on reaching the free air, he let it out with a yell loud enough to have been heard a mile off, and then began, tied up as he was, to shout for joy as I supported him to the shore.

'After this happy deliverance, we immediately began our search for your dead body, Ralph, and you have no idea how low our hearts sank as we set off, day after day, to examine the valleys and mountain sides with the utmost care. In about three weeks we completed the survey of the whole island, and had at least the satisfaction of knowing that you had not been killed. But it occurred to us that you might have been thrown into the sea, so we examined the sands and the lagoon carefully, and afterwards went all round the outer reef. One day, while we were upon the reef, Peterkin espied a small dark object lying among the rocks, which seemed to be quite different from the surrounding stones. We found it to be a small keg. It was gunpowder.'

'It was I who sent you that, Jack,' said I, with a smile, explaining how the thing had occurred.

'Well, we found it very useful,' continued Jack; 'although some of it had got a little damp; and we furbished up the old pistol, with which Peterkin is a crack shot now. But, to continue. We finally gave up all hope of ever seeing you again. After this the island became a dreary place to us, and we began to long for a ship to heave in sight and take us off. But now that you're back again, it looks as bright and cheerful as it used to do, and I love it as much as ever. And now,' continued Jack, 'I have a great desire to visit some of the other islands of the South Seas. Here we have a first-rate schooner at our disposal, so I don't see what should hinder us.'

'Just the very thing I was going to propose,' cried Peterkin; 'I vote for starting at once.'

'Well, then,' said Jack, 'it seems to me that we could not do better than shape our course for the island on which Avatea lives, and endeavour to persuade Tararo to let her marry the black fellow to whom she is engaged, instead of making a long pig of her. If he has a spark of gratitude in him he'll do it. Besides, having become champions for this girl once before, it behoves us, as true knights, not to rest until we set her free.'

Having made up his mind to save this black girl, Jack could not rest until the thing was commenced.

'But there may be great danger in this attempt,' he said, at the end of a long consultation on the subject. 'Will you lads go with me in spite of this?'

'Go with you?' we repeated in the same breath.

We lost no time in making preparations to quit the island; and as the schooner was well laden with stores of every kind for a long cruise, we had little to do except to add a quantity of coconuts, bread-fruit, taro, yams, plums, and potatoes.

When all was ready, we paid a farewell visit to the different familiar spots where most of our time had been spent.

Last of all, we returned to the bower and collected the few articles we possessed, such as the axe, the pencil-case, the broken telescope, the penknife, the hook made from the brass ring, and the sail-needle, with which we had landed on the island – also, the long boots and the pistol, besides several curious articles of costume which we had manufactured from time to time.

These we conveyed on board in our little boat, after having carved our names on a chip of iron-wood, thus:

JACK MARTIN

RALPH ROVER

PETERKIN

which we fixed up inside the bower. The boat was then hoisted on board and the anchor weighed. A steady breeze was blowing off-shore when we set sail a little before sunset. It swept us quickly past the reef and out to sea. The shore grew rapidly more indistinct while our clipper bark bounded lightly over the waves. Slowly the mountain-top sank on the horizon, until it became a mere speck. In another moment the sun and the Coral Island sank together into the Pacific.

CHAPTER XIV

Our voyage during the next two weeks was most interesting and prosperous. The breeze continued generally fair, and at all times enabled us to lie our course. We had no difficulty now in managing our sails, for Jack was heavy and powerful, while Peterkin was active as a kitten. We nevertheless found that my pulleys were of much service to us in some things; though Jack did laugh heartily at the uncouth arrangement of ropes and blocks, which had, to a sailor's eye, a very lumbering and clumsy appearance. After an agreeable sail of about three weeks, we arrived off the island of Mango, which I recognized at once from the description that the pirate, Bill, had given me of it.

As soon as we came within sight of it we hove the ship to, and held a council of war.

'Now, boys,' said Jack, as we seated ourselves beside him on the cabin skylight, 'before we go farther in this business, we must go over the pros and cons of it. Now, I understand from you, Ralph, that the island is inhabited by thorough-going, out-and-out cannibals, whose principal law is: "Might is right, and the weakest goes to the wall"?'

'Yes,' said I, 'so Bill gave me to understand. He told me, however, that, at the southern side of it, the missionaries had obtained a footing amongst an insignificant tribe. A native teacher had been sent there by the Wesleyans, who had succeeded in persuading the chief at that part to embrace Christianity. But instead of that being of any advantage to our enterprise, it seemed the very reverse; for the chief Tararo is a determined heathen, and persecutes the Christians – who are far too weak in numbers to offer any resistance – and looks with dislike upon all white men.'

' 'Tis a pity,' said Jack, 'that the Christian tribe is so small, for we shall scarcely be safe under their protection, I fear. If Tararo takes it into his head to wish for our vessel, or to kill us, he could take us by force. You say that the native missionary talks English?'

'So I believe.'

'Then, what I propose is this,' said Jack. 'We will run round to the south side of the island, and cast anchor off the Christian village. But we run the risk of being captured by the ill-disposed tribes, and being very ill-used, if not – a –'

'Roasted alive and eaten,' cried Peterkin. 'Come out with it, Jack; it's well to look the danger straight in the face!'

'Well, that *is* the worst of it, certainly. Are you prepared, then, to take your chance of that?'

'I had my mind made up long ago,' cried Peterkin, swaggering about the deck with his hands thrust into his breeches' pockets. 'The fact is, Jack, I don't believe that Tararo will be so ungrateful as to eat us; and I'm quite sure that he'll be too happy to grant us whatever we ask: so the sooner we go in and win the better.'

Peterkin was wrong, however, in his estimate of savage gratitude.

The schooner was now put before the wind, and, after making a long run to the south'ard, we put about and beat up for the south side of Mango, where we arrived before sunset, and hove-to off the coral reef. Here we awaited the arrival of a canoe, which immediately put off on our rounding to. When it arrived, a mild-looking native, of apparently forty years of age, came on board, and, taking off his straw hat, made us a low bow. He was clad in a respectable suit of European clothes; and the first words he uttered, as he stepped up to Jack and shook hands with him, were: 'Good day, gentlemen; we are happy to see you at Mango – you are heartily welcome.'

After returning his salutation, Jack exclaimed: 'You must be the native missionary teacher of whom I have heard – are you not?'

'I am. I have the joy to be a servant of the Lord Jesus at this station.'

'You're the very man I want to see, then,' replied Jack; 'that's lucky. Come down to the cabin, friend, and have a glass of wine. I wish particularly to speak with you. My men there' – pointing to Peterkin and me – 'will look after your people.'

'Thank you,' said the teacher, as he followed Jack to the cabin, 'I do not drink wine or any strong drink.'

'Oh! then, there's lots of water, and you can have a biscuit.'

'Now, 'pon my word, that's cool!' said Peterkin. 'His *men*, forsooth! Well, since we are to be men, we may as well come it as strong over these black chaps as we can. Hallo, there!' he cried to the half-dozen natives who stood upon the deck, gazing in wonder at all they saw, 'here's for you;' and he handed them a tray of broken biscuit and a can of water. Then, thrusting his hands into his pockets, he walked up and down the deck with an enormous swagger.

In about half an hour Jack and the teacher came on deck, and the latter, bidding us a cheerful good evening, entered his canoe and paddled to the shore. When he was gone, Peterkin stepped up to Jack, and, touching his cap, said: 'Well, captain, have you any communications to make to your *men*?'

'Yes,' cried Jack; 'ready about, and mind the helm while I con the schooner through the passage in the reef. The teacher, who seems a first-rate fellow, say it's quite deep, and good anchorage within the lagoon close to the shore.'

While the vessel was slowly advancing to her anchorage, under a light breeze, Jack explained to us that Avatea was still on the island, living among the heathens; that she had expressed a strong desire to join the Christians, but Tararo would not let her, and kept her constantly in close confinement.

'Moreover,' continued Jack, 'I find that she belongs to one of the Samoan Islands, where Christianity had been introduced long before her capture by the heathens of a neighbouring island. The teacher tells me, too, that the poor girl has fallen in love with a Christian chief, who lives on an island some fifty miles or so to the south of this one, and that she is meditating a desperate attempt at escape. So, you see, we have come in the nick of time. I fancy that this chief is the fellow whom you heard of, Ralph, at the Island of Emo. Besides all this, the heathens are at war among themselves, and there's to be a battle fought the day after tomorrow, in which the principal leader is Tararo; so that we'll not be able to commence our negotiations with the rascally chief till the day after.'

The village off which we anchored was beautifully situated at the head of a small bay, from the margin of which trees of every description peculiar to the tropics rose in the richest luxuriance to the summit of a hilly ridge, which was the line of demarcation between the possessions of the Christians and those of the neighbouring heathen chief.

The site of the settlement was an extensive plot of flat land, stretching in a gentle slope from the sea to the mountain. The cottages stood several hundred yards from the beach, and were protected from the glare of the sea by the rich foliage of rows of large trees, which girt the shore. The village was about a mile in length, and perfectly straight, with a wide road down the middle, on either side of which were rows of the tufted-topped ti tree, whose delicate and beautiful blossoms added richness to the scene. The cottages were built beneath these trees, and were kept in the most excellent order, each having a little garden in front, while the walks were covered with black and white pebbles.

Every house had doors and Venetian windows, painted partly with lamp black made from the candle-nut, and partly with red ochre, which contrasted powerfully with the dazzling coral lime that covered the walls. On a prominent position stood a handsome church, which was quite a curiosity in its way. It was a hundred feet long by fifty broad, and could seat upwards of two thousand persons. It had six large folding doors and twelve windows with Venetian blinds; and, although a large and substantial edifice, it had been built, we were told by the teacher, in the space of two months! There was not a single iron nail in the fabric, and the natives had constructed it chiefly with their stone and bone axes and other tools. Everything around this beautiful spot wore an aspect of peace and plenty, and, as we dropped our anchor within a stone's cast of the substantial coral wharf, I could not avoid contrasting it with the wretched village of Emo, where I had witnessed so many frightful scenes.

On landing from our little boat, we were received with a warm welcome by the teacher and his wife, the latter being also a native, clothed in a simple European gown and straw bonnet. The shore was lined with hundreds of natives, whose persons were all more or less clothed with native cloth. Some of the men had on a kind of poncho formed of this cloth, their legs being uncovered. Others wore clumsily fashioned trousers, and no upper garment except hats made of straw and cloth. They seemed very glad to see us, and crowded round us as the teacher led the way to his dwelling, where we were entertained, in the most sumptuous manner, on baked pig and all the varieties of fruits and vegetables that the island produced. We were much annoyed, however, by the rats: they seemed to run about the house like domestic animals. As we sat at table, one of them peeped up at us over the edge of the cloth, close to Peterkin's elbow, who floored it with a blow on the snout from his knife, exclaiming as he did so: 'I say, Mister Teacher, why don't you set traps for these brutes? Surely you are not fond of them!'

'No,' replied the teacher with a smile; 'we would be glad to get rid of them if we could; but if we were to trap all the rats on the island, it would occupy our whole time.'

We had not been an hour in the house of this kind-hearted man when we were convinced of the truth of his statement as to their numbers, for the rats ran about the floors in dozens, and, during our meal, two men were stationed at the table to keep them off!

'What a pity you have no cats,' said Peterkin, as he aimed a blow at another reckless intruder, and missed it.

'We would, indeed, be glad to have a few,' rejoined the teacher, 'but they are difficult to be got. The hogs, we find, are very good rat-killers, but they do not seem to be able to keep the numbers down. I have heard that they are better than cats.'

Next day we walked out with this interesting man, and were much entertained by his conversation, as we rambled through the cool shady groves of bananas, citrons, limes, and other trees, or sauntered among the cottages of the natives, and watched them while they laboured diligently in the taro beds, or manufactured the tapa or native cloth. To some of these Jack put questions through the medium of the missionary; and the replies were such as to surprise us at the extent of their knowledge. Indeed, Peterkin very truly remarked that 'they seemed to know a considerable deal more than Jack himself!'

The missionary gave us an account of the manner in which Christianity had been introduced among them. He said: 'When missionaries were first sent here, three years ago, a small vessel brought them; and the chief, who is now dead, promised to treat well the two native teachers who were left with their wives on the island. But scarcely had the boat which landed them returned to the ship, than the natives began to maltreat their guests, taking away all they possessed, and offering them further violence, so that, when the boat was sent in haste to fetch them away, the clothes of both men and women were torn nearly off their backs.

'Two years after this the vessel visited them again, and I, being in her, volunteered to land alone, without any goods whatever; begging that my wife might be brought to me the following year – that is, *this* year; and, as you see, she is with me. But the surf was so high that the boat could not land me; so with nothing on but my trousers and shirt, and with a few catechisms and a Bible, besides some portions of the Scripture translated into the Mango tongue, I sprang into the sea, and swam ashore on the crest of a breaker. I was instantly dragged up the beach by the natives; who, on finding I had nothing worth having upon me, let me alone. I then made signs to my friends in the ship to leave me; which they did. At first the natives listened to me in silence, but laughed at what I said while I preached the gospel of our blessed Saviour Jesus Christ to them. Afterwards they treated me ill sometimes; but I persevered, and continued to dwell among them, and exhort them to give up their sinful ways of life, burn their idols, and come to Jesus.

'About a month after I landed, I heard that the chief was dead. He was the father of the present chief, who is now a most consistent member of the church. It is a custom here that, when a chief dies, his wives are strangled and buried with him. Knowing this, I hastened to his house to endeavour to prevent such cruelty if possible. When I arrived, I found two of the wives had already been killed, while another was in the act of being strangled. I pleaded hard for her, but it was too late; she was already dead. I then entreated the son to spare the fourth wife; and, after much hesitation, my prayer was granted: but, in half an hour afterwards, this poor woman repented of being unfaithful, as she termed it, to her husband, and insisted on being strangled; which was accordingly done.

'All this time the chief's son was walking up and down before his father's house with a brow black as thunder. When he entered, I went in with him, and found, to my surprise, that his father was *not* dead! The old man was sitting on a mat in a corner, with an expression of placid resignation on his face.

'"Why," said I, "have you strangled your father's wives before he is dead?"

'To this the son replied: "He is dead. That is no longer my father. He is as good as dead now. He is to be *buried alive*."

'I now remembered having heard that it is a custom among the Fiji islanders, that when the reigning chief grows old or infirm, the heir to the chieftainship has a right to depose his father; in which case he is considered as dead, and is buried alive. The young chief was now about to follow this custom, and, despite my earnest entreaties and pleadings, the old chief was buried that day before my eyes in the same grave with his four strangled wives! Oh! my heart groaned when I saw this, and I prayed to God to open the hearts of these poor creatures, as he had already opened mine, and pour into them the light and the love of the gospel of Jesus. My prayer was answered very soon. A week afterwards, the son, who was now chief of the tribe, came to me, bearing his god on his shoulders, and groaning beneath its weight. Flinging it down at my feet, he desired me to burn it!

'You may conceive how overjoyed I was at this. I sprang up and embraced him. Then we made a fire, and burned the god to ashes, amid an immense concourse of the people, who shrank back when we burned the god, expecting some vengeance to be taken upon us; but seeing that nothing happened, they changed their minds, and thought that our God must be the true one after all. From that time the mission prospered steadily. You see,' he said, waving his hand around him, 'the village and the church did not exist a year ago!'

We were indeed much interested in this account. The teacher also added that the other tribes were very indignant at this for having burned its god, and threatened to destroy it altogether, but they had done nothing yet; 'and if they should,' said the teacher, 'the Lord is on our side; of whom shall we be afraid?'

On returning towards the village, about noon, we remarked on the beautiful whiteness of the cottages.

'That is owing to the lime with which they are plastered,' said the teacher. 'When the natives were converted I set them to work to build cottages for themselves, and also this handsome church. When the framework and other parts of the houses were up, I sent the people to fetch coral from the sea. They brought immense quantities. Then I made them cut wood, and, piling the coral above it, set it on fire.

'"Look! look!" cried the poor people, in amazement; "what wonderful people the Christians are! He is roasting stones. We shall not need taro or bread-fruit any more; we may eat stones!''

'But their surprise was still greater when the coral was reduced to fine soft white powder. They immediately set up a great shout, and, mingling the lime with water, rubbed their faces and their bodies all over with it, and ran through the village screaming with delight.

As the teacher concluded this anecdote we reached his door. Saying that he had business to attend to, he left us to amuse ourselves as we best could.

'Now, lads,' said Jack, turning abruptly towards us, and buttoning up his jacket as he spoke, 'I'm off to see the battle. I've no particular fondness for seein' bloodshed, but I must find out the nature o' these fellows and see their customs with my own eyes. It's only six miles off, and we don't run much more risk than that of getting a rap with a stray stone or an overshot arrow. Will you go?'

'To be sure we will,' said Peterkin.

We had ascertained from the teacher where the battle was to be fought, and after a walk of two hours reached it. The summit of a bare hill was the place chosen. We arrived before the two parties had commenced the deadly struggle, and, creeping as close up as we dared among the rocks, we lay and watched them.

The combatants were drawn up face to face, each side ranged in rank four deep. Those in the first row were armed with long spears; the second, with clubs to defend the spear-men; the third row was composed of young men with slings; and the fourth consisted of women, who carried baskets of stones for the slingers, and clubs and spears with which to supply the warriors. Soon after we arrived, the attack was made with great fury. There was no science displayed. The two bodies of natives rushed headlong upon each other and engaged in a general mêlée, and a more dreadful set of men I have never seen. They wore grotesque war-caps decorated with feathers. Their faces and bodies were painted so as to make them look as frightful as possible; and they brandished their massive clubs, leaped, shouted, yelled, and dashed each other to the ground.

We were much surprised at the conduct of the women, who seemed to be perfect furies, and hung about the heels of their husbands in order to defend them. But the battle did not last long. The band most distant from us gave way and were routed, leaving eighteen of their comrades dead upon the field. These the victors brained as they lay; and putting some of their brains on leaves went off with them, we were afterwards informed, to their temples, to present them to their gods.

We hastened back to the Christian village with feelings of the deepest sadness.

Next day, after breakfasting with our friend the teacher, we made preparations for carrying out our plan. At first the teacher endeavoured to dissuade us.

'You do not know,' said he, turning to Jack, 'the danger you are running in venturing amongst these ferocious savages. I feel much pity for poor Avatea; but you are not likely to succeed in saving her, and you may die in the attempt.'

'Well,' said Jack, quietly, 'I am not afraid to die in a good cause.'

The teacher smiled approvingly at him as he said this, and agreed to accompany us as interpreter; saying that, although Tararo was unfriendly to him, he had hitherto treated him with respect.

We now went on board the schooner, having resolved to sail round the island and drop anchor opposite the heathen village. We manned her with natives, and hoped to overawe the savages by displaying our brass gun to advantage. The teacher soon after came on board, and setting our sails we put to sea. In two hours more we made the cliffs reverberate with the crash of the big gun, which we fired by way of salute, while we ran the British ensign up to the peak and cast anchor. The commotion on shore showed us that we had

175

struck terror into the hearts of the natives; but seeing that we did not offer to molest them, a canoe at length put off and paddled cautiously towards us. The teacher showed himself, and explaining that we were friends and wished to palaver with the chief, desired the native to go and tell him to come on board.

We waited long and with much impatience for an answer. During this time the native teacher told us many things concerning the success of the gospel among those islands. Jack seemed deeply impressed, and wore an anxious expression on his naturally grave countenance, while he put many earnest questions to the teacher. Meanwhile the natives who composed our crew had squatted down on the deck and taken out their little books containing the translated portions of the New Testament, along with hymns and spelling-books, and were now busily engaged, some learning prayers off by heart, while a few sang hymns – all of them being utterly unmindful of our presence. The teacher joined them, and soon afterwards they all engaged in a prayer for the success of our undertaking and for the conversion of the heathen.

While we were thus engaged a canoe put off from shore and several natives leaped on deck, one of whom advanced to the teacher and informed him that Tararo could not come on board that day, being busy with some religious ceremonies which could on no account be postponed. He was also engaged with a friendly chief who was about to take his departure from the island, and therefore begged that the teacher and his friends would land and pay a visit to him. To this the teacher returned answer that we would land immediately.

'Now, lads,' said Jack, as we were about to step into our little boat, 'I'm not going to take any weapons with me, and I recommend you to take none either. We are altogether in the power of these natives, and the utmost we could do, if they were to attack us, would be to kill a few of them before we were ourselves overpowered. I think that our only chance of success lies in mild measures. Don't you think so?'

To this I assented gladly, and Peterkin replied by laying down a huge bell-mouthed blunderbuss, and divesting himself of a pair of enormous horse-pistols with which he had purposed to overawe the natives! We then jumped into our boat and rowed ashore.

On reaching the beach we were received by a crowd of naked men, who shouted a rude welcome, and conducted us to a house or shed where a baked pig and a variety of vegetables were prepared for us. Having partaken of these, the teacher begged to be conducted to the chief; but there seemed some hesitation, and after some consultation among themselves, one of the men stood forward and spoke to the teacher.

'What says he?' enquired Jack.

'He says that the chief is just going to the temple of his god and cannot see us yet; so we must be patient, my friend.'

'Well,' cried Jack, rising; 'if he won't come to see me, I'll e'en go and see him. Besides, I have a great desire to witness their proceedings at this temple of theirs. Will you go with me, friend?'

'I cannot,' said the teacher, shaking his head; 'I must not go to the heathen temples and witness their inhuman rites, except for the purpose of condemning their wickedness and folly.'

'Very good,' returned Jack; 'then I'll go alone, for I cannot condemn their doings till I have seen them.'

Jack arose, and we followed him through the banana groves to a rising ground immediately behind the village, on the top of which stood the *Buré*, or temple, under the dark shade of a group of iron-wood trees. As we went through the village, I was again led to contrast the rude huts and sheds, and their almost naked savage-looking inhabitants, with the natives of the Christian village.

As we turned into a broad path leading towards the hill, we were arrested by the shouts of an approaching multitude in the rear. Drawing aside into the bushes we awaited their coming up, and observed that it was a procession of the natives, many of whom were dancing and gesticulating in the most frantic manner. They had an exceedingly hideous aspect owing to the black, red, and yellow paints with which their faces and naked bodies were bedaubed. In the midst of these came a band of men carrying three or four planks, on which were seated in rows upwards of a dozen men. I shuddered involuntarily as I recollected the sacrifice of human victims at the island of Emo, and turned with a look of fear to Jack as I said: 'Oh, Jack! I have a terrible dread that they are going to commit some of their cruel practices on these wretched men. We had better not go to the temple. We shall only be horrified without being able to do any good, for I fear they are going to kill them.'

Jack's face wore an expression of deep compassion as he said, in a low voice: 'No fear, Ralph; the sufferings of these poor fellows are over long ago.'

I turned with a start as he spoke, and, glancing at the men saw that they were all dead. They were tied firmly with ropes in a sitting posture on the planks, and seemed, as they bent their sightless eyeballs and grinning mouths over the dancing crew below, as if they were laughing in ghastly mockery at the utter inability of their enemies to hurt them now. These, we discovered afterwards, were the men who had been slain in the battle of the previous day, and were now on their way to be first presented to the gods, and then eaten. Behind these came two men leading between them a third, whose hands were pinioned behind his back. He walked with a firm step, and wore a look of utter indifference on his face; so that we concluded he must be a criminal who was about to receive some slight punishment for his faults. The rear of the procession was brought up by a shouting crowd of women and children, with whom we mingled and followed to the temple.

The temple was a tall circular building, open at one side. Around it were strewn heaps of human bones and skulls. At a table inside sat the priest, an elderly man, with a long grey beard. He was seated on a stool, and before him lay several knives, made of wood, bone, and splinters of bamboo, with which he performed his office of dissecting dead bodies. Farther in lay a variety of articles that had been dedicated to the god, and among them were many spears and clubs.

Before this temple the bodies, which were painted with vermilion and soot, were arranged in a sitting posture; and a man, called a *dan-vosa* (orator), advanced, and, laying his hands on their heads, began to chide them, apparently, in a low bantering tone. What he said we knew not, but he at last shouted at them at the top of his lungs, and finally finished by kicking the bodies over and running away, amid the shouts and laughter of the people, who now rushed forward. Seizing the bodies by a leg, or an arm, or by the hair of the head, they dragged them over stumps and stones and through sloughs, until they were exhausted. The bodies were then brought back to the temple and dissected by the priest, after which they were taken out to be baked.

Close to the temple a large fire was kindled, in which stones were heated red hot. When ready these were spread out on the ground, and a thick coating of leaves strewn over them to slack the heat. On this 'lovo,' or oven, the bodies were then placed, covered over, and left to bake.

The crowd now ran, with terrible yells, towards a neighbouring hill or mound, on which we observed the framework of a house lying ready to be erected. Sick with horror, yet fascinated by curiosity, we staggered after them.

Arrived at the place, we saw the multitude crowding round a certain spot. We pressed forward and obtained a sight of what they were doing. A large wooden beam or post lay on the ground, beside the other parts of the framework of the house, and close to the end of it was a hole about seven feet deep and upwards of two feet wide. While we looked, the man whom we had before observed with his hands pinioned, was carried into the circle. His hands were now free, but his legs were tightly strapped together. The post of the house was then placed in the hole, and the man put in beside it. His head was a good way below the surface of the hole, and his

arms were clasped round the post. Earth was now thrown in
until all was covered over and stamped down; and this, we
were afterwards told, was a *ceremony* usually performed at the
dedication of a new temple, or the erection of a chief's house!

'Come, come,' cried Jack, on beholding this horrible trage-
dy, 'we have seen far more than enough! Let us go.'

Jack's face looked ghastly pale and haggard as we hurried
back to rejoin the teacher, and I have no doubt that he felt
terrible anxiety when he considered the number and ferocity
of the savages, and the weakness of the few arms which were
impotent to effect Avatea's deliverance from these ruthless
men.

CHAPTER XV

When we returned to the shore, and related to our friend what had passed, he was greatly distressed, and groaned in spirit; but we had not sat long in conversation, when we were interrupted by the arrival of Tararo on the beach, accompanied by a number of followers bearing baskets of vegetables and fruits on their heads.

We advanced to meet him, and he expressed, through our interpreter, much pleasure in seeing us.

'And what is it that my friends wish to say to me?' he enquired.

The teacher explained that we came to beg that Avatea might be spared.

'Tell him,' said Jack, 'that I consider that I have a right to ask this of him, having not only saved the girl's life, but the lives of his own people also; and say that I wish her to be allowed to follow her own wishes, and join the Christians.'

While this was being translated, the chief's brow lowered, and we could see plainly that our request met with no favourable reception. He replied with considerable energy, and at some length.

'What says he?' enquired Jack.

'I regret to say that he will not listen to the proposal. He says he has pledged his word to his friend that the girl shall be sent to him, and a deputy is even now on this island awaiting the fulfilment of the pledge.'

Jack bit his lip in suppressed anger. 'Tell Tararo,' he exclaimed with flashing eye, 'that if he does not grant my demand, it will be worse for him! Say I have a big gun on board my schooner that will blow his village into the sea, if he does not give up the girl.'

'Nay, my friend,' said the teacher, gently, 'I will not tell him that; we must "overcome evil with good."'

'What does my friend say?' enquired the chief.

'He is displeased,' replied the teacher.

Tararo turned away with a smile of contempt, and walked towards the men who carried the baskets of vegetables, and who had now emptied the whole on the beach in an enormous pile.

'What are they doing there?' I enquired.

'I think that they are laying out a gift which they intend to present to someone,' said the teacher.

At this moment a couple of men appeared leading a young girl between them; and, going towards the heap of fruits and vegetables, placed her on the top of it. We started with surprise and fear, for in the young female before us we recognized the Samoan girl, Avatea!

We stood rooted to the earth with surprise and fear.

'Oh! my dear young friends,' whispered the teacher, in a voice of deep emotion, while he seized Jack by the arm, 'she is to be made a sacrifice even now!'

'Is she?' cried Jack, with a vehement shout, pushing the teacher aside, and dashing over two natives who stood in his way, while he rushed towards the heap, and seized Avatea by the arm. In another moment he dragged her down, placed her back to a large tree, and, wrenching a war-club from the hand of a native who seemed powerless and petrified with surprise, whirled it above his head, and yelled, rather than shouted, while his face blazed with fury: 'Come on, the whole nation of you, and do your worst!'

It seemed as though the challenge had been literally accepted; for every savage on the ground ran precipitately at Jack with club and spear, and, doubtless, would speedily have poured out his brave blood on the sod, had not the teacher rushed in between them, and, raising his voice to its utmost, cried: 'Stay your hands, warriors! It is for Tararo, the chief, to say whether or not the young man shall live or die.'

The natives were arrested; and I know not whether it was

some lingering feeling of gratitude for Jack's former aid in time of need that influenced Tararo, but he stepped forward, and, waving his hand, said to his people: 'Desist. The young man's life is mine.' Then, turning to Jack, he said: 'You have forfeited your liberty and life to me. Submit yourself, for we are more numerous than the sand upon the shore. You are but one; why should you die?'

'Villain!' exclaimed Jack, passionately. 'I may die, but, assuredly, I shall not perish alone. I will not submit until you promise that this girl shall not be injured.'

'You are very bold,' replied the chief, haughtily, 'but very foolish. Yet I will say that Avatea shall not be sent away, at least for three days.'

'You had better accept these terms,' whispered the teacher, entreatingly. 'If you persist in this mad defiance, you will be slain, and Avatea will be lost. Three days are worth having.'

Jack hesitated a moment, then lowered his club, crossed his arms on his breast, and hung his head in silence.

Tararo seemed pleased by his submission, and told the teacher to say that he did not forget his former services, and, therefore, would leave him free, but that the schooner would be detained till he had further considered the matter.

While the teacher translated this, he approached as near to Avatea as possible, without creating suspicion, and whispered to her a few words in the native language. Avatea replied by a single rapid glance of her dark eyes, which were instantly cast down again on the ground at her feet.

Tararo now advanced, and taking the girl by the hand, led her unresistingly away, while Jack, Peterkin, and I returned with the teacher on board the schooner.

We went down to the cabin, where Jack threw himself, in a state of great dejection, on a couch; but the teacher seated himself by his side, and said: 'Do not give way to anger, my young friend. God has given us three days. We must not sit in idle disappointment, we must act –'

'Act!' cried Jack, raising himself, and tossing back his hair wildly. 'How can I act? I cannot fight a whole nation of savages single-handed. Yes,' he said, with a bitter smile, 'I *can* fight them, but I cannot conquer them, or save Avatea.'

'Patience, my friend. I will tell you my plans if you will listen.'

'Listen!' cried Jack, eagerly. 'Of course I will, my good fellow; I did not know you had any plans. Out with them. I only hope you will show me how I can get the girl on board this schooner, and I'd up anchor and away in no time. But proceed with your plans.'

The teacher smiled sadly. 'Ah! my friend, if one fathom of your anchor chain were to rattle, as you drew it in, a thousand warriors would be standing on your deck. No, no, that could not be done. Even now, your ship would be taken from you were it not that Tararo has some feeling of gratitude towards you. But I know Tararo well. He is a man of falsehood. The chief to whom he has promised this girl is very powerful, and Tararo *must* fulfil his promise. He has told you that he would do nothing to the girl for three days; but that is because the party who are to take her away will not be ready to start for three days. Still, as he might have made you a prisoner during those three days, I say that God has given them to us.'

'Well, but what do you propose to do?' said Jack, impatiently.

'My plan involves much danger, but I see no other, and I think you have courage to brave it. It is this. There is an island about fifty miles to the south of this, the natives of which are Christians, and have been so for two years or more, and the principal chief is Avatea's lover. Once there, Avatea would be safe. Now, I suggest that you should abandon your schooner. Do you think that you can make so great a sacrifice?'

'Friend,' replied Jack, 'when I make up my mind to go through with a thing of importance, I can make any sacrifice.'

The teacher smiled. 'Well, then, the natives could not

conceive it possible that, for the sake of a girl, you would voluntarily lose your fine vessel; therefore as long as she lies here they think they have you all safe: so I suggest that we get a quantity of stores conveyed to a sequestered part of the shore, provide a small canoe, put Avatea on board, and you three would paddle to the Christian island.'

'Bravo!' cried Peterkin, springing up and seizing the teacher's hand. 'Missionary, you're a regular brick.'

'As for me,' continued the teacher, 'I will remain on board till they discover that you are gone. Then they will ask me where you are gone to, and I will refuse to tell.'

'And what'll be the result of that?' enquired Jack.

'I know not. Perhaps they will kill me; but I too am not afraid to die in a good cause!'

'But how are we to get hold of Avatea?' enquired Jack.

'I have arranged with her to meet us at a particular spot, to which I will guide you tonight. She will easily manage to elude her keepers, who are not very strict in watching her, thinking it impossible that she could escape from the island. But you run great danger. Fifty miles in a small canoe, on the open sea, is a great voyage to make. You may miss the island, too, in which case there is no other in that direction for a hundred miles or more. You must count the cost, my young friend.'

'I have counted it,' replied Jack. 'If Avatea consents to run the risk, most certainly I will; and so will my comrades also.'

We now set about active preparations for the intended voyage; collected together such things as we should require, and laid out on the deck provisions sufficient to maintain us for several weeks, purposing to load the canoe with as much as she could hold consistent with speed and safety. These we covered with a tarpaulin, intending to convey them to the canoe only a few hours before starting. When night came we prepared to land; but, first, kneeling along with the natives and the teacher, the latter implored a blessing on our enterprise. Then we rowed quietly to the shore and followed our sable guide, who led us by a long detour, in order to avoid the village, to the place of rendezvous. We had not stood more than five minutes under the gloomy shade of the thick foliage when a dark figure glided noiselessly up to us.

'Ah! here you are,' said Jack, as Avatea approached. 'Now, then, tell her what we've come about, and don't waste time.'

'I understan' leetl English,' said Avatea, in a low voice.

'Why, where did you pick up English?' exclaimed Jack, in amazement. 'You were dumb as a stone when I saw you last.'

'She has learned all she knows of it from me,' said the teacher, 'since she came to the island.'

We now gave Avatea a full explanation of our plans, concealing none of the danger, so that she might be fully aware of the risk she ran. She was too glad of the opportunity to escape from her persecutors to think of the danger or risk.

'Then you're willing to go with us, are you?' said Jack.

'Yis, I am willing to go.'

'And you're not afraid to trust yourself out on the deep sea so far?'

'No, I not 'fraid to go. Safe with Christian.'

After some further consultation, we bade Avatea good night, and having appointed to meet at the cliff where the canoe lay, on the following night, just after dark, we hastened away – we to row on board the schooner with muffled oars, Avatea to glide back to her prison hut.

As the time for our flight drew near, we became very fearful lest our purpose should be discovered, and spent the whole of the following day in a state of nervous anxiety. We resolved to go ashore and ramble about the village, as if to observe the habits and dwellings of the people, as we thought that an air of affected indifference to the events of the previous day would avert suspicion as to our intentions.

At last the long and tedious day came to a close, and the short-lived twilight of those regions ended abruptly in a dark night. Hastily throwing a few blankets into our little boat, we stepped into it, and rowed gently over the lagoon, taking care to keep as near to the beach as possible. We rowed in the utmost silence and with muffled oars. Not a breath of air was stirring; but fortunately the gentle ripple of the sea upon the shore, mingled with the soft roar of the breaker on the distant reef, effectually drowned the slight splash that we made in the water by the dipping of our oars.

Quarter of an hour sufficed to bring us to the overhanging cliff under whose black shadow our little canoe lay, with her bow in the water ready to be launched, and most of her cargo already stowed away. As the keel of our little boat grated on the sand, a hand was laid upon the bow, and a dim form was seen.

'Ha!' said Peterkin in a whisper. 'Is that you, Avatea?'

'Yis, it am me,' was the reply.

'All right! Now, then, gently. Help me to shove off the canoe,' whispered Jack to the teacher. 'Avatea, step into the middle – that's right.'

'Is all ready?' whispered the teacher.

'Not quite,' replied Peterkin. 'Here, Ralph, lay hold o' this pair of oars, and stow them away if you can. I don't like paddles.'

One more earnest squeeze of the kind teacher's hand, and we shot like an arrow from the shore, sped over the still waters of the lagoon, and paddled as swiftly as strong arms and willing hearts could urge us over the long swell of the open sea.

All that night and the whole of the following day we plied our paddles in almost total silence and without halt, save twice to recruit our failing energies with a mouthful of food and a draught of water. Jack had taken the bearing of the island just after starting, and laying a small pocket-compass before him, kept the head of the canoe due south, for our chance of hitting the island depended very much on the faithfulness of our steersman in keeping our tiny bark exactly on its proper course. Peterkin and I paddled in the bow, and Avatea worked untiringly in the middle.

As the sun dipped on the gilded edge of the sea Jack ceased working, threw down his paddle, and called a halt.

'There,' he cried, heaving a deep, long-drawn sigh, 'we've put a considerable breadth of water between us and these black rascals, so now we'll have a hearty supper and a sound sleep.'

'Hear, hear,' cried Peterkin. 'Nobly spoken, Jack. Hand me a drop of water, Ralph. Why, girl, what's wrong with you? You look just like a black owl blinking in the sunshine.'

Avatea smiled. 'I sleepy,' she said; and as if to prove the truth of this, she laid her head on the edge of the canoe and fell fast asleep.

'That's uncommon sharp practice,' said Peterkin, with a broad grin. 'Don't you think we should awake her to make her eat something first? Or, perhaps,' he added, with a grave, meditative look, 'perhaps we might put some food in her mouth, which is so elegantly open at the present moment, and see if she'd swallow it while asleep.'

I could not help smiling at Peterkin's idea, which, indeed, when I pondered it, seemed remarkably good in theory; nevertheless I declined to put it in practice, being fearful of the result should the victual chance to go down the wrong throat. But, on suggesting this to Peterkin, he exclaimed: 'Down the wrong throat, man! Why, a fellow with half an eye might see that if it went down Avatea's throat it could not go down the wrong throat! However, hand me the pork before Jack finishes it. I feel myself entitled to at least one minute morsel. I say, Ralph, do leave just one little slice of that yam. Between you and Jack I run a chance of being put on short allowance, if not – yei – a – a – ow!'

Peterkin's concluding remark was a yawn of so great energy that Jack recommended him to postpone the conclusion of his meal till next morning.

We lay like a shadow on the ocean, while the night closed in, and all around was calm, dark, and silent.

A cry of alarm from Peterkin startled us in the morning, just as dawn began to glimmer in the east.

'What's wrong?' cried Jack, starting up.

Peterkin replied by pointing with a look of anxious dread towards the horizon. One of the largest sized war-canoes was approaching us!

With a groan of despair Jack seized his paddle, glanced at the compass, and commanded us to 'give way.' But we did not require to be urged. Already our four paddles were glancing in the water, and the canoe bounded over the glassy sea like a dolphin, while a shout from our pursuers told that they had seen us.

'I see something like land ahead,' said Jack, in a hopeful tone. 'It seems impossible that we could have made the island yet; still, if it is so, we may reach it before these fellows can catch us, for our canoe is light and our muscles are fresh.'

No one replied; for we felt that in a long chase we had no chance whatever with a canoe which held nearly a hundred warriors. Nevertheless, we resolved to do our utmost to escape, and paddled with a degree of vigour that kept us well in advance of our pursuers. The war-canoe was so far behind us that it seemed but a little speck on the sea. We therefore hoped that we should be able to keep in advance for an hour or two, when we might, perhaps, reach the land ahead. But this hope was suddenly crushed by the supposed land, not long after, rising up into the sky, thus proving itself to be a fog-bank!

A bitter feeling of disappointment filled each heart. But we had little time to think of regret. Our danger was too great. A feeling of despair, strange to say, lent us power to work, and nerved our arms with such energy, that it was several hours before the natives overtook us. When we saw that there was indeed no chance of escape, and that paddling any longer would only serve to exhaust our strength, without doing any good, we turned the side of our canoe towards the approaching enemy, and laid down our paddles.

Silently, and with a look of bitter determination on his face, Jack lifted one of the light boat-oars that we had brought with us, and, resting it on his shoulder, stood up in

189

an attitude of bold defiance. Peterkin took the other oar and also stood up. He glanced at Avatea, who sat with her face resting in her hands upon her knees. Without knowing very well what I intended to do, I also arose and grasped my paddle with both hands.

On came the large canoe like a war-horse of the deep, with the foam curling from its sharp bow, and the spearheads of the savages glancing in the beams of the rising sun. Perfect silence was maintained on both sides, and we could hear the hissing water, and see the frowning eyes of the warriors, as they came rushing on. When about twenty yards distant, five or six of them rose, and laying aside their paddles, took up their spears. Jack and Peterkin raised their oars, while I grasped my paddle and prepared for the onset. But, before any of us could strike a blow, the sharp prow of the war-canoe struck us like a thunderbolt on the side, and hurled us into the sea!

What occurred after this I cannot tell, for I was nearly drowned; but when I recovered I found myself stretched on my back, bound hand and foot between Jack and Peterkin, in the bottom of the large canoe.

In this condition we lay the whole day, during which time the savages only rested one hour. When night came, they rested again for another hour, and appeared to sleep just as they sat. But we were neither unbound nor allowed to speak to each other during the voyage, nor was a morsel of food or a draught of water given to us. For food, however, we cared little; but we would have given much for a drop of water, and we would have been glad, too, had they loosened the cords that bound us, for they were tightly fastened and occasioned us much pain. The air, also, was unusually hot, so much so that I felt convinced that a storm was brewing. This also added to our sufferings. However, these were at length relieved by our arrival at the island from which we had fled.

While we were being led ashore, we caught a glimpse of Avatea, who was seated in the hinder part of the canoe. She was not fettered in any way. Our captors now drove us before them towards the hut of Tararo, at which we speedily arrived, and found the chief seated with an expression on his face that boded us no good. Our friend the teacher stood beside him, with a look of anxiety on his mild features.

'How comes it,' said Tararo, turning to the teacher, 'that these youths have abused our hospitality?'

'Tell him,' replied Jack, 'that we have not abused his hospitality, for his hospitality has not been extended to us. I came to the island to deliver Avatea, and my only regret is that I have failed to do so. If I get another chance, I will try to save her yet.'

On hearing Jack's speech, Tararo frowned and his eye flashed with anger.

'Go,' he said, 'presumptuous boy. My debt to you is cancelled. You and your companions shall die.'

As he spoke he rose and signed to several of his attendants, who seized Jack and Peterkin and me violently by the collars, and led us through the wood to the outskirts of the village. Here they thrust us into a species of natural cave in a cliff, and, having barricaded the entrance, left us in total darkness.

After feeling about for some time – for our legs were unshackled, although our wrists were still bound with thongs – we found a low ledge of rock running along one side of the cavern. On this we seated ourselves, and for a long time maintained unbroken silence.

At last I could restrain my feelings no longer. 'Alas!' said I 'What is to become of us? I fear that we are doomed to die.'

'I know not,' replied Jack, in a tremulous voice. 'Perhaps the teacher may do something for us. But I have little hope.'

'Ah! no,' said Peterkin, with a heavy sigh; 'I am sure he can't help us. Tararo doesn't care more for him than for one of his dogs.'

'Truly,' said I, 'there seems no chance of deliverance. Yet I must say that I have great hope, my comrades, for we have come to this dark place by no fault of ours – unless it be a fault to try to succour a woman in distress.'

I was interrupted in my remarks by a noise at the entrance to the cavern, which was caused by the removal of the barricade. Immediately after, three men entered, and led us away through the forest. As we advanced, we heard much shouting and beating of native drums in the village, and at first we thought that our guards were conducting us to the hut of Tararo again. But in this we were mistaken. The beating of drums gradually increased, and soon after we observed a procession of the natives coming towards us. At the head of this procession we were placed, and then we all advanced together towards the temple where human victims were sacrificed!

Horror ran through my heart as I recalled the awful scenes that I had before witnessed at that dreadful spot. But deliverance came suddenly from a quarter whence we little expected it. During the whole of that day there had been an unusual degree of heat in the atmosphere, and the sky assumed that lurid aspect which portends a thunderstorm. Just as we were approaching the temple, a growl of thunder burst overhead and heavy drops of rain began to fall.

Those who have not witnessed gales and storms in tropical regions can form but a faint conception of the fearful hurricane that burst upon the island of Mango at this time. Before we reached the temple, the storm burst upon us with a deafening roar, and the natives, who knew too well the devastation that was to follow, fled right and left through the woods in order to save their property, leaving us alone in the midst of the howling storm. The trees around us bent before the blast like willows, and we were about to flee in order to seek shelter, when the teacher ran towards us with a knife in his hand.

'Thank the Lord,' he said, cutting our bonds, 'I am in time! Now, seek the shelter of the nearest rock.'

This we did without a moment's hesitation, for the whistling wind burst like thunderclaps among the trees, and tearing them from their roots, hurled them with violence to the ground. Rain cut across the land in sheets, and lightning played like forked serpents in the air; while, high above the roar of the hissing tempest, the thunder crashed and rolled in awful majesty.

In the village the scene was absolutely appalling. Roofs were blown completely off the houses in many cases; and in others, the houses themselves were levelled with the ground. In the midst of this the natives were darting to and fro, in some instances saving their goods, but in many others seeking to save themselves from the storm of destruction that whirled around them. But, terrific although the tempest was on land, it was still more tremendous on the mighty ocean. Billows sprang, as it were, from the great deep, and fell upon the beach with a crash that seemed to shake the solid land. But they did not end there. Each successive wave swept higher and higher on the beach, until the ocean at length, in a sheet of white curdled foam, swept into the village and upset and carried off, or dashed into wreck, whole rows of the native dwellings! It was an awful scene.

We found shelter in a cave that night and all the next day, during which time the storm raged in fury; but on the night following it abated somewhat, and in the morning we went to the village to seek for food, being so famished with hunger that we lost all feeling of danger. But no sooner had we obtained food than we began to wish that we had rather endeavoured to make our escape into the mountains. This we attempted to do soon afterwards, but we were seized by three warriors, who once more bound our wrists and thrust us into our former prison.

CHAPTER XVI

For a long, long month we remained in our dark and dreary prison, during which dismal time we did not see the face of a human being, except that of the silent native who brought us our daily food.

During the first part of our confinement we felt a cold chill at our hearts every time we heard a footfall near the cave – dreading lest it should prove to be that of our executioner. But as time dragged heavily on, we ceased to feel this alarm, and began to experience such a deep, irrepressible longing for freedom, that we chafed and fretted in our confinement like tigers.

A few decayed leaves and boughs formed our bed; and a scanty supply of yams and taro, brought to us once a day, constituted our food.

'Well, Ralph, how have you slept?' said Jack, in a listless tone one morning. 'Were you much disturbed by the wind last night?'

'No,' said I; 'I dreamed of home all night.'

'And I dreamed, too,' said Peterkin; 'but it was of our happy home on the Coral Island. I thought we were swimming in the Water Garden.'

We sat for some time in deep silence. Soon after, we heard footsteps at the entrance of the cave, and immediately our jailer entered. We were so much accustomed to his regular visits, however, that we paid little attention to him, expecting that he would set down our meagre fare, as usual, and depart. But, to our surprise, instead of doing so, he advanced towards us with a knife in his hand, and, going up to Jack, he cut the thongs that bound his wrists, then he did the same to Peterkin and me! For fully five minutes we stood in speechless amazement, with our freed hands hanging idly by our sides. The first thought that rushed into my mind was that the time had come to put us to death.

But I was mistaken. After cutting our bonds, the native pointed to the cave's mouth, and we marched into the open air. Here, to our surprise, we found the teacher standing under a tree, with his hands clasped before him, and the tears trickling down his dark cheeks. On seeing Jack, who came out first, he sprang towards him, and exclaimed: 'Oh! my dear young friend, through the great goodness of God you are free!'

'Free!' cried Jack.

'Ay, free,' repeated the teacher, shaking us warmly by the hands again and again; 'free to go and come as you will. A missionary has been sent to us, and Tararo has embraced the Christian religion! The people are even now burning their gods of wood! Come, my dear friends, and see the glorious sight.'

We could scarcely credit our senses. Our eyes and minds were dazzled, too, by the brilliant sunshine after our long confinement to the gloom of our prison, so that we felt giddy; but as we followed the footsteps of our sable friend, and heard the cries of the parakeets, and smelt the rich perfume of the flowering shrubs, the truth rushed with overwhelming power into our souls, and with one accord we uttered a loud long cheer of joy.

It was replied to by a shout from a number of the natives who chanced to be near. Running towards us, they shook us by the hand with every demonstration of kindly feeling. They then conducted us to the dwelling of Tararo.

The scene that met our eyes here was one that I shall never forget. On a rude bench in front of his house sat the chief. A native stood on his left hand, who, from his dress, seemed to be a teacher. On his right stood an English gentleman, who, I at once and rightly concluded, was a missionary. He was tall, thin, and apparently past forty, with a bald forehead, and thin grey hair. His clear grey eyes beamed with a look that was frank, fearless, and truthful. In front of the chief was an open space, in the centre of which lay a pile of wooden idols, ready to be set on fire; and around these were assembled thousands of natives, who had come to witness the unusual sight. A bright smile overspread the missionary's face as he shook us warmly by the hands.

'I am overjoyed to meet you, my dear young friends,' he said. 'My friend, and *your* friend, the teacher, has told me your history; and I thank our Father in heaven that He has guided me to this island, and made me the instrument of saving you.'

We thanked the missionary most heartily, and asked him in some surprise how he had succeeded in turning the heart of Tararo in our favour.

'I will tell you that at a more convenient time,' he answered; 'meanwhile we must not forget the respect due to the chief. He wants to receive you.'

In the conversation between us and Tararo, the latter said that the light of the gospel of Jesus Christ had been sent to the island, and that to it we were indebted for our freedom. Moreover, he told us that we were at liberty to depart in our schooner whenever we pleased, and that we should be supplied with as much provision as we required. He concluded by shaking hands with us warmly, and performing the ceremony of rubbing noses.

This was indeed good news to us, and we could hardly find words to express our gratitude to the chief and to the missionary.

'And what of Avatea?' enquired Jack.

The missionary replied by pointing to a group of natives in the midst of whom the girl stood. Beside her was a tall, strapping fellow, whose noble mien and air of superiority bespoke him a chief of no ordinary kind.

'That youth is her lover. He came this very morning in his war-canoe to treat with Tararo for Avatea. He is to be married in a few days, and afterwards returns to his island home with his bride!'

'That's capital,' said Jack, as he stepped up to the native and gave him a hearty shake of the hand. 'I wish you joy, my lad – and you too, Avatea.'

As Jack spoke, Avatea's lover took him by the hand and led him to the spot where Tararo and the missionary stood, surrounded by most of the chief men of the tribe. The girl herself followed, and stood on his left hand while her lover stood on his right, and, commanding silence, made the following speech, which was translated by the missionary:

'Young friend, you have seen few years, but your head is old. Your heart is very brave. I and Avatea are your debtors, and we wish to acknowledge our debt, and to say that it is one which we can never repay. We, who live in these islands of the sea, know that the true Christians always act thus. Their religion is one of love and kindness. Remember that I and Avatea will think of you and pray for you and your brave comrades when you are far away.'

To this kind speech Jack returned a short sailor-like reply. But Jack's forte did not lie in speech-making, so he terminated rather abruptly by seizing the chief's hand and shaking it violently, after which he made a hasty retreat.

'Now, then, Ralph and Peterkin,' said Jack, as we mingled with the crowd, 'it seems to me that the object we came here for having been satisfactorily accomplished, we have nothing more to do but get ready for sea as fast as we can, and hurrah for dear old England!'

'That's my idea precisely,' said Peterkin. 'However, I'm not going away till I see these fellows burn their gods.'

Peterkin had his wish, for in a few minutes fire was put to the pile, the roaring flames ascended, and, amid the acclamations of the assembled thousands, the false gods of Mango were reduced to ashes!

The time soon drew near when we were to quit the islands of the South Seas; and, strange though it may appear, we felt deep regret at parting with the natives of the island of Mango; for, after they embraced the Christian faith, they sought, by showing us the utmost kindness, to compensate for the harsh treatment we had experienced at their hands; and we felt a growing affection for the native teachers and the missionary, and especially for Avatea and her husband.

During the short time that we remained at the island, repairing our vessel and getting her ready for sea, the natives had commenced building a large and commodious church, under the superintendence of the missionary, and several rows of new cottages were marked out; so that the place bid fair to become, in a few months, as prosperous and beautiful as the Christian village at the other end of the island.

After Avatea was married, she and her husband were sent away, loaded with presents, chiefly of an edible nature. One of the native teachers went with them, for the purpose of visiting still more distant islands of the sea, and spreading, if possible, the light of the gospel there.

As the missionary intended to remain for several weeks longer, Jack and Peterkin and I held a consultation in the cabin of our schooner – which we found just as we had left her, for everything that had been taken out of her was restored. We resolved to delay our departure no longer. The desire to see our beloved native land was strong upon us, and we could not wait.

Three natives volunteered to go with us to Tahiti, where we thought it likely that we should be able to procure a sufficient crew of sailors to man our vessel; so we accepted their offer gladly.

It was a bright clear morning when we hoisted the snow-white sails of the pirate schooner and left the shores of Mango. The missionary, and thousands of the natives, came down to bid us God-speed. As the vessel bent before a light fair wind, we glided quickly over the lagoon under a cloud of canvas.

Just as we passed through the channel in the reef the natives gave us a loud cheer; and as the missionary waved his hat, while he stood on a coral rock with his grey hairs floating in the wind, we heard the single word 'Farewell' borne faintly over the sea.

That night, as we sat on the taffrail, gazing out upon the wide sea and up into the starry firmament, a thrill of joy, strangely mixed with sadness, passed through our hearts – for we were at length 'homeward bound,' and were leaving far behind us the beautiful bright green coral islands of the Pacific Ocean.

You can see more Magnet Books on the following pages

STEPHANIE CONELL AND DIANE STOKER

Rainbow Books of Fun Things To Do

An exciting series of activity books exploring all kinds of ideas from the popular television programme, *Rainbow*. With the help of Zippy, Bungle and George and simply written instructions, children will love to learn new ideas and activities.

The first three titles in the series are:
Puppets
Dressing Up
Messy Things
Illustrated in full colour by Joan Hickson

ANDREW DAVIES

Marmalade Atkins in Space

Some people think Marmalade Atkins is the worst girl in the world; Sister Purification and Sister Conception, who have to teach her think so; Cherith Ponsonby, headgirl of the Convent, thinks so; the staff of the El Poko Nightclub think so; even her parents think so.

Mrs Allgood, who is in the Helping Professions, knows the answer: Very Extreme Treatment. In VET, Bad Girls are sent off into space to be turned into Goody-Goodies. But has Mrs Allgood met her match in Marmalade?

Based on the Thames TV Theatrebox Production

JAN NEEDLE

Wild Wood

Wild Wood tells the story of Brotherhood Hall – Toad Hall as it is more usually known – through the sharp and penetrating memory of an ancient and helpful ferret. Cedric Willoughby, driving his 1907 Armstrong Hardcastle Mouton Special Eight in the London to Brighton Veteran Car Run, crashes in a lonely spot and is rescued by elderly Baxter Ferret, who as well as repairing the car, tells him the story of Toad's extravagant escapades and the invasion of Toad Hall from the Wild Wooders' point of view.

This ingenious narrative is neither parody nor satire, though it contains obvious elements of both; it is in no way a sequel to *Wind in the Willows* but stands entirely on its own – in many ways a celebration of Kenneth Grahame's masterpiece.

'I enjoyed every word, and only partly because I had loved the *Wind in the Willows*.'
The Daily Telegraph

MAX FATCHEN

The River Kings

Shawn runs away from a harsh stepfather to take a job on a riverboat, trading on the Murray River in Australia at the turn of the century.

Conquest of the River

The second exciting adventure of Shawn and the crew of the *River Queen* as they face a terrible flood.

Chase Through the Night

Three men on the run after a hold-up take as hostages Petra Gwinson and her sick mother, and abduct them to a tiny outback settlement in Australia's Northern Territory. But the robbers haven't counted on the setbacks everyone makes for them.

The Spirit Wind

Life was harsh aboard the *Hootzen*, an old squarerigger bound for Australia at the turn of the century. Once in port, Jarl deserted and became a hunted man. But Nunganee, the old Aborigine, helped him by raising the spirit wind.

MONICA HUGHES

Crisis on Conshelf Ten

When Kepler Masterman visits Earth for the first time, he finds heavy gravity impossible to live in. An underwater atmosphere seems to offer the best solution to his problems, and friendly relatives welcome him to their experimental community under the ocean, many fathoms deep. But on Conshelf Ten Kepler discovers a sinister situation linked to the mysterious, water-breathing Gillmen, and realises that not only is he in great personal danger but the survival of the entire Earth is threatened.

'Strangely convincing.'   *Daily Telegraph*
'An excellent story.'   *The Times*

MONICA HUGHES

Earthdark

Returning to the Moon after an exciting visit to Earth, Kepler Masterman finds life back home frustratingly sterile. The well-ordered, utilitarian society on the Moon contrasts grimly with the freedom and fun he experienced on Earth.

Desperate for adventure Kepler decides to take a forbidden trip out on to the Moon's surface but even he did not bargain for the sinister series of events which he finds himself caught up in. Narrowly escaping death, he returns to Base only to find that his girlfriend's father has disappeared. Fearing for his safety, the two set out for the strange and unknown region of Earthdark on the farthest side of the Moon where they believe Ann's father may be. But something important is taking place in Earthdark – something which interests more than one ruthless power – and unaware of the dangerous forces surrounding them, the young people walk straight into a trap . . .

MONICA HUGHES

The Keeper of the Isis Light

When a group of settlers from Earth land on the beautiful planet of Isis they arrive to a world completely uninhabited except by Olwen, Keeper of the Isis Light and her protector, Guardian. Olwen is nervous about what the newcomers will think of her and frustrated when Guardian insists that she put on a germ-free suit before she descends to the valley where they are camped. Down there Mark London quickly befriends the masked Olwen and she learns how much pleasure there is in human friendship, though there are also bitter disappointments. She is ultimately to find out that she and this alien planet are uniquely linked.

These and other Magnet Books are available at your bookshop or newsagent. In case of difficulties, orders may be sent to:

Magnet Books
Cash Sales Department
PO Box 11
Falmouth
Cornwall TR10 9EN
England

Please send cheque or postal order, no currency, for purchase price quoted and allow the following for postage and packing:

U.K. CUSTOMERS
40p for the first book, plus 18p for the second book and 13p for each additional book ordered, to a maximum charge of £1.49.

BFPO & EIRE
40p for the first book, plus 18p for the second book and 13p per copy for the next 7 books, thereafter 7p per book.

OVERSEAS CUSTOMERS
60p for the first book, plus 18p per copy for each additional book.

While every effort is made to keep prices low, it is sometimes necessary to increase prices at short notice. Magnet Books reserve the right to show new retail prices on covers which may differ from those previously advertised in the text or elsewhere.